SILINSKI
Master Criminal

By EDGAR WALLACE

MYSTERY LIBRARY

THE WORLD SYNDICATE PUBLISHING CO.
CLEVELAND, O.   NEW YORK, N. Y.

Printed in the United States of America

CONTENTS

CONTENTS

SILINSKI
Master Criminal

SILINSKI
Master Criminal
By EDGAR WALLACE

CHAPTER I

ECLIPSE

Men who think in millions, usually pay in installments, but this was not the case with Silinski, who had a mind for small things, and between whiles, when mighty financial schemes were not occupying the screen, had time to work out his landlady's bill and detect the altogether fallacious addition of

	3 peseta 25 centimos.
	4 ” 50 ”
as	8 peseta 75 centimos.

He might, indeed, have hailed from Andalusia as did the Senora with her thrifty additions and her buxom red and white and black beauty, for he counted his pennies carefully and never received a duoro without testing it with his teeth.

He was a tall man with a stoop, and dressed invariably in black, which is the colour of Spain. Seeing him, on windy days, when bleak, icy airstreams poured down from the circling Sierras, and made life in Madrid insupportable, you might have marked him down as a Spaniard. His black felt hat and his velvet-lined cappa with its high collar would show him to be such from a distance, whilst nearer at hand, his long, melancholy face, with a thin nose that drooped over a trim black moustache slightly upturned, would confirm the distant impression. He spoke Spanish fluently, and affected a blazing diamond ring—such as a well-to-do Spaniard would delight in.

Silinski was, in fact, a Pole, and had been for many years a patriot, finding the calling lucrative.

Of all the bad men of whose history I have knowledge, or whose acquaintance I have made, none more than Silinski looked the part.

He was the transpontine villain to the life, and is the only instance I can recall of such a creature. He was in appearance so clever, so cunning, so snake-like, suave, and well-mannered, that men, and not a few women, trusted him from sheer perversity, reasoning, no doubt, that no man who looked so utterly untrustworthy could be anything but good at bottom. Reflecting on the bad men I have known, I enter into the spirit of the reasoning. Jan Muller was benevolent of face, with a kindly eye that twinkled behind gold-rimmed spectacles—yet Muller's record is known, and for the five murders that were brought home to him, a score were undiscovered. Bawker had the face of a clown, a weak, good-natured clown, with his loose lip and the puckered eyes of a lover of good living —Bawker was a cold-hearted murdered. Agma Cymon—I doubt if that was his real name—was a cold severe, just man, infinitely precise and methodical; a mean man who would fight over a penny, and who invariably had his clothing patched, and his shoes re-soled, yet Cymon's defalcations amounted to £127,000, and the bulk of the money went to the upkeep of an establishment over which the beautiful Madame Carron-Setter presided.

Silinski looked what he was, yet people did not shake their heads over him. Rather they received him in their homes, and some, more intimately acquainted, joked with him on his Mephistophelian ensemble.

Silinski came to Burgos, from Madrid, by an excursion train that travelled all night, yet he was the trimmest and most alert of the crowd which thronged the Callo do Vitoria, a crowd made up of peasants, tourists, and soldiers.

He made slow progress, for the crowd grew thicker in the vicinity of the Casa del Cordon, where the loyal country-folk waited patiently for a glimpse of their King.

Silinski stood for a little while looking up at the expressionless windows of the Casa, innocent of curtain, but strangely clean. He speculated on the value of life—of royal life.

"If I were to kill the King," he mused, "Europe would dissolve into one big shudder. If, being dead, I came forward offering to restore him to life for fifty million francs the money would be instantly forthcoming on the proof of my ability. Yet were I to go now to the King's minister saying—'It is easy for me to kill the King, but if you will give me the money you would spend on his obsequies. I will stay my hand,' I should be kicked out, arrested, and possibly confined as a lunatic."

He nodded his head slowly, and as he turned away he took a little notebook from his pocket, and inscribed—"The greatest of miracles is self-restraint." Then he rolled a cigarette and walked slowly back to the Cafè Suiso in the Espollon.

A clean-shaven priest, with a thin, intellectual face, was stirring his coffee at one of the tables, and since this was the least occupied Silinski made for it. He raised his hat to the priest and sat down.

"I apologize for intruding myself, father," he said, "but the other tables——"

The priest smiled and raised a protesting hand.

"The table is at your disposition, my son," he said.

He was about the same age as Silinski, but he spoke with the assurance of years. Silinski noted that the priest's voice was modulated, his accent refined, his presence that of a gentleman.

"A Jesuit," thought Silinski, and regarded him with politely veiled curiosity. Jesuits had a fascination for him. They were clever, and they were good; but principally they were a mysterious force that rode triumphant over the prejudice of the world and the hatred in the Church.

"If I were not an adventurer," he said aloud, and with that air of simplicity which ever proved to be his most valuable asset, "I should be a Jesuit."

The priest smiled again, looking at Silinski with calm interest.

"My son," he said, "if I were not a Jesuit priest, I should be suspicious of your well-simulated frankness."

Here would have come a deadlock to a man of lesser parts than Silinski, but he was a very adaptable man. None the less, he was surprised into a laugh which showed his white teeth.

"In Spain," he said, "no gambit to conversation is known. I might have spoken of the weather, of the crowd, of the King—I chose to voice my faults."

The priest shook his head, still smiling.

"It is of no importance," he said quietly, "you are a Pole, of course?"

Silinski stared at him blankly. These Jesuits—strange stories had been told about them. A body with a secret organization, spread over the world —it had been said that they were hand-in-hand with the police.

"I knew you were a Pole; I lived for some time in Poland. Besides, you are only Spanish to your feet," the Jesuit looked down at Silinski's boots, "they are not Spanish; they are too short and too heavy."

Silinski laughed again. After all, this was a confirmation of his views of Jesuits.

"You, my father," he accused in his turn, "are a teacher; a professor at the college in Madrid; a professor of languages," he stopped and looked up to the awning that spread above him, seeking inspiration. "A professor of Greek," he said slowly.

"Arabic," corrected the other, "but that deduction isn't clever, because the Jesuits at Madrid are all engaged in scholastic work."

"But I knew you came from Madrid," smiled Silinski.

"Because we both came by the same train," said the calm priest, "and for the same purpose."

Silinski's eyes narrowed.

"For what purpose, father?" he asked.

"To witness the eclipse," said the priest.

A few minutes later, Silinski watched the black-robed figure with the broad-rimmed hat disappearing in the crowd with a little feeling of irritation.

He had not come to Burgos to witness the eclipse of the sun, but because he knew that the phenomenon would attract to the ancient stronghold of the Cid many notabilities. Notabilities were usually rich men, and these Silinski was anxious to meet. A Spanish gentleman, who could speak fluently French, English, German, and Italian, might, if he played his cards well, secure introductions at such a time as this, which ordinarily would be out of his reach. The guarded circles of Paris and London, through which the unknown could not hope to penetrate, would be assailable here.

A stately Spanish grandee (which was Silinski's role) might call on my lord in Berkeley Square, and receive no happier welcome than the suspicious scrutiny of an under footman. His ability to speak English would not serve him in a city where 6,000,000 of people spoke it indifferently well.

Silinski had come to Burgos as another man might go to a horse fair, in the hope of picking up a bargain; only, in the case of the Pole, it was a human bargain he desired, a profitable investment which he could secure for a hundred pesetas—for that was the exact amount of capital he at the moment controlled.

So with Silinski in Burgos, with crowds hurrying to the hill above the cathedral to witness the eclipse, and with no other actor in this strange drama upon the stage, the story of the Nine Bears begins.

Silinski scrawled a platitude in his notebook— had it been an epigram I would have recorded it— drank the remainder of his *café au lait,* signed to the waiter and paid him the exact amount due. Leaving the outraged servant speechless, he stepped into the stream and was swept up the hill to where a number of English people were gathered, with one eye upon their watches and another upon the livid shadow that lay upon the western sky.

Silinski found a place on the slope of the hill tolerably clear of sightseers, and spread a handkerchief carefully on the bare baked earth and sat down. He had invested a penny in a strip of smoked glass, and through this he peered critically at the sun. The hour of contact was at hand, and he could see the thin rim of the obstruction cover the edge of the glaring ball.

He had all the clever man's respect for the astuteness of the scientist, and as he waited he wondered by what method astronomers were able to so accurately fortell to the minute, to the second, nay to the thousandth part of a second, the time of eclipse. Perhaps—

"Say, this place will do, it's not so crowded."

Silinski looked up at the newcomers.

One was short and stout and breathed stertorously, having recently climbed the hill, the other, the speaker, was tall, well-groomed and unmistakably an American, with his rimless glasses and his square-toed boots.

"Phew!" wheezed the fat man. "Don't know which was worse, the climb or the crowd." He tapped his inside pocket apprehensively. "Hate crowds," he grumbled, "lose things."

"Have you lost anything?" asked the other.
The fat man shook his head, but felt his pocket
again. Silinski saw this out of the corner of his
eye—inside breast pocket on the left, he noted.

"Baggin," said the fat man suddenly, "I've a
feelin' that we oughtn't to have come here."

"You make me tired," said the American wearily.

"We oughtn't to be seen together," persisted
the other; "all sorts of people are here, eh? Fellers I know slightly, chaps in the City, eh? They'll
smell a rat."

He was querulous and worrying, and had a
trick of asking for corroboration where none was
likely to be offered.

"You're a fool," said the other.

There was a long pause, and Silinski knew that
the American was making dumb show signals of
warning. They were nodding at him, he felt sure,
so he raised his hat and asked politely:

"At what hour is the eclipse?"

"No savvy," said the fat man, "no hablo es-
pagnol."

Silinski shrugged his shoulders, and turned
again to the contemplation of the plain below.

"He doesn't speak English," said the fat man,
"none of these beggars do."

The American made no reply, but after a silence of a few minutes, he said quietly and in English: "Look at that balloon."

But Silinski was too experienced a warrior to be trapped by a simple trick like that, and continued his solid regard of the landscape; besides, he had seen the balloons parked on the outskirts of the town, and knew that intrepid scientists would make the ascent to gather data.

He took another look at the sun. The disc was half-way across its surface, and the west was grey and blue, and the little clouds that flecked the sky were iridescent. Crowds still poured up the hill, and the slope was now covered with people. He had to stand up, and in doing so he found himself side by side with the fat man.

A strange light was coming to the world; there were triple shadows on the ground, and the stout man, whose name was Meyers, shifted uneasily.

"Don't like this, Baggin," he said fretfully; "it's hateful—never did like these wonders of the sky, they make me nervous—am frightened, Baggin, eh? It's awful, it's damned awful. Look out there, out west behind you, eh? It's black, black— it's like the end of the world!"

"Cut it out!" said his unimaginative companion.

Then of a sudden the black shadow in the west leaped across the sky, and the world went grey black. Where the sun had been was a hoop of fire, a bubbling, boiling circle of golden light, and the circling horizon was a dado of bright yellow. It was as though the sun had set at its zenith, and the sunset glows were shown, east, west, north, and south.

"My God! My God!" the fat man shook in his terror; "it's horrible, horrible."

He covered his face with his hands, oblivious to everything, save a gripping fear of the unknown that clawed at his heart.

He was blind and deaf to the hustling, murmuring crowd about him; only he knew he stood in the darkness at high noon, and that something was happening he could not compress within the limits of his understanding.

Three minutes the eclipse lasted, then, as suddenly as it began, it ended.

A blazing, blinding wave of light flooded the world, and the stars that had studded the sky went out.

"Yes—yes, I know I'm a fool." His face was bathed in perspiration, although with the darkness had come the chill of death. "It's—it's my

temperament, eh? But never again! It's an experience.''

He shook his head, as his trembling legs carried
him down the hillside; then he tapped his pocket
mechanically and stopped dead.

"Gone!" he gasped, and dived into his pocket.
"Gone! by hell!" he roared. "Fifty thousand
francs—gone—I've been robbed, Baggin——''

"You must expect that sort of thing in a
crowd.'' said the philosophical American.

*　　*　　*

Silinski went into the cathedral to count the
money—it was very quiet in the cathedral.

CHAPTER II

SILINSKI HAS A PLAN

Silinski had a sister who was beautiful. She enjoyed a vogue in Madrid as Foudonitya, a great dancer. She went her own way, having no reason for showing respect for her brother, or regard for his authority. This did not greatly exercise Silinski. But her way—so easy a way!—led to outrageous unconventionalities, and there were certain happenings which need not be particularized. She was solemnly excommunicated by the Archbishop of Toledo, and the evening newspapers published her photograph.

Silinski was annoyed.

"Child," he had said gravely to her, "you did wrong to come into conflict with the Church."

"It will be a good advertisement," she said.

Silinski shook his head, and said nothing.

That night Foudonitya was hissed off the stage of the Casino, and came to her brother, not weeping or storming, but philosophically alarmed.

"What am I to do?" she asked.

22

"Go away into the country and perform good works; be kind to the poor, hire a duenna, and make the acquaintance of the local correspondent of the *Heraldo de Madrid*."

"It will cost money," said the practical Catherine—this was her name.

"You can do nothing without money," said Silinski, and would have entered the saying in his notebook, but for the fact that it sounded trite.

So Catherine went into the country, and from time to time there appeared notes of her charity in the Madrid papers. She was still in the country when the ban of excommunication was withdrawn and she did penance at Cordova.

Silinski was not greatly surprised to see her dining at the Hotel de Paris at Burgos, on the night of the eclipse, but her hosts—they could not be her guests, for Catherine was one of the frugal sort—gave him occasion for thought. He stood in the doorway watching them. He had been looking for an empty table when he saw Catherine, and after a first glance he would have turned and departed, waiting until his sister was disengaged, but the fat man saw him.

"Hi!" he bellowed, "there he is—stop him, somebody!"

Silinski required no stopping; rather he came

forward with a smile, offering his hand to the beautiful girl.

"That was the fellow who was standing near me when I lost the money," fumed the fat man, and looked helplessly round for a policeman.

There was a scraping of chairs, a confusion of voices; people rose from their seats craning their necks in an endeavour to secure a better view of what was happening, in the midst of which Mr. Meyers found himself pulled to his chair.

"Keep quiet—you," hissed Baggin's voice in his ear; "you fool, you're getting exactly a million dollars' worth of the wrong kind of publicity —he knows the girl." He leaned across the table and smiled crookedly at Silinski. "Sit down, won't you? My friend thinks he knows you—introduce us, Senora."

The commotion died down as it had begun, occasional curious glances being thrown at the strange quartette.

"Your brother?" Baggin looked keenly at the bowing stranger. "Well, we've met him before, and my friend entertained rather unjust suspicions—but they were preposterous, of course."

Silinski bowed again with a grave and patient smile.

"He didn't understand English on the hill, eh?"

Meyers choked as his suspicions found fresh food. "Don't like it Baggin, don't *like* it, I tell you!" He had a trick of dropping pronouns, which gave his speech an extraordinary rapidity of utterance.

"We had the pleasure of meeting your sister in Ronda a few weeks ago," Baggin went on smoothly, and Silinski nodded. He did not ask by what means this prosperous-looking American had secured an introduction in this land of punctilio. On Catherine's hand blazed a ring he had not remembered seeing before. "As we are leaving Spain tomorrow, we offered her a parting feast—"

He was feeling his way with Silinski, not quite sure of his ground. Silinski might be the outraged relative, the proud hidalgo, quickly and easily affronted, terrible in his vengeance. The girl needed some explaining away.

As for Silinski, did Baggin but know, the girl had explained her presence when she laid her hand on the white table-cloth and the fires of her ring leaped and fell in the gas-light.

"Senor," said Silinski benevolently, "I am gratified beyond measure with your courtesy. We Bohemians, we artists, ask nor offer excuse for our departures from the convention. My little one"—he patted Catherine's white hand—

"makes friends quickly, but"—here he shrugged his shoulders and turned a pained face to the wheezing Mr. Meyers—"some observations have been made which reflect upon my honour."

"No offence," growled Meyers sulkily.

"Pardon," Silinski raised his hand, dignity and respect in every pose, "pardon, Senor, I could not fail to comprehend your accusation. I stood by your side on the hill, so absorbed, so rapt in the glories of the phenomena, that I could not bring my elated mind to the level of understanding." He resolved to remember this phrase. "I understood nothing, heard nothing, saw nothing, but the astral splendour——"

"No offence, no offence," grumbled the fat man, "didn't think before I spoke; worried, worried, worried!" He waggled his fat hand to and fro as though illustrating the process of perturbation.

"As to that," said Silinski, with a magnificent sweep of hand, "we agree to forget; but you lost money——"

"Lost money!" the fat man glared, "lost more than money, important documents, eh? Precioco—precious, savvy? Letter from feller in the city, no possible value except to owner, see?"

"Let us go on with our dinner," said Baggin roughly; "you talk too much, Louis."

"Letters have been lost, seemingly, irredeemably lost," persisted Silinski, who was not at all anxious to change the subject, "yet, by such agencies as I have at present in my mind, have been restored to their grateful and generous owners."

"Detectives, eh?" Meyers' glare was now ferocious. "Spyin', pryin', lyin' detectives? *No!* by—"

Baggin looked across at the girl in patient despair.

"I was not thinking of detectives—by the way, Burgos seems filled with these gentlemen," Silinski went on. "I was thinking of a genius who makes this country his home. His name"—Silinski's voice was emphatic as he created from his mind the wonderful investigator— "his name is Senor don Sylvester de Gracia, and he is a personal friend of mine."

"Oh! let the thing go," interrupted Baggin impatiently. "You've lost it, and there's an end to it; the thief will be satisfied with the money and tear the letter up."

"Unless," mused Silinski, "the thief is arrested by the police, and the letter is found upon him. Then the authorities might send for Senor T. B. Smith—eh?"

Meyers' face went ashen, and his thick lips began to quiver like a child on the point of crying.

"Smith? T. B. Smith? Commissioner, Scotland Yard! Not here, eh? Damn it, he's not here!"

"I passed him in the Plaza Mayos less than an hour ago; a gentleman very easily amused."

"Smith!" Meyers' shaking hand poured out a glass of amber wine. "Bah! mistaken!"

"I know him slightly," said Silinski modestly (it was T. B. Smith who had marked him for deportation under the Undesirable Aliens Act); "I never forget a face."

The fat man pushed back his chair, wiping his big mouth clumsily with a serviette.

"Then it's *up,*" he said. "He's here for something; my name's Mud in the city——"

"Be quiet!" Baggin turned with a snarl upon his companion. "Look here," he said, facing Silinski, "my friend is not quite himself—I'll take him up to my room for a minute or so; will you wait here? You might be of service to us."

Without waiting for an answer the two men left the room, Baggin with one hand clenched on the fat man's arm.

When they had gone Silinski turned to his sister.

"I hope you haven't scared them," she said in German.

"I think not," said her amiable relative, and the two exchanged confidences.

"What have they done?" she asked.

"Nothing—as yet," he said diplomatically.

"You have this letter?" she asked, but Silinski shook his head.

"If I had," he said, "I could tell you all you want to know. Unfortunately I am in the dark."

"And the money?"

"I know no more about the money than you," he replied, with charming frankness. "Who are they?"

She laughed, showing two straight, white rows of teeth, and there was genuine amusement in her big grey eyes. "You have the money, of course, and the letter—you must tell me, Gregory. I must know where I am with them; it is due to me."

"As to the money," said Silinski, without shame, "it is some fifty thousand francs; one might live for a year in luxury upon fifty thousand francs. As for the letter—why, that is an annuity forever."

He leaned over the table, and as he looked his eyes were lowered to the cloth, like a man ransacking his memory for elusive facts.

"These men are part of an epidemic—a wave of financial instability is rushing across the world—

no, I will put it inimitably: There are props of rotten finance; sometimes one pole snaps and the structure trembles, sometimes two snap and the structure lurches, but does not fall, for there is strength in union, and it is more difficult to break a bundle of worm-eaten sticks than one honest stave. But suppose all the props are withdrawn at once—what happens? Ph-tt! And suppose the weaker props say—'The big fellow is going—it is time for us to move'?"

Catherine listened patiently.

"I would rather you spoke less like a priest, in parables," she said.

"Naturally," said Silinski, with an easy inclination of his head, as though this were the very comment he expected, "yet I must deal in parables. Amongst your accomplishments, do you speak English?"

"A little." Catherine shrugged her shoulders carelessly. "I can say 'my dear' and 'I like you very much'."

"Which hardly fulfils all commercial requirements," said Silinski thoughtfully. "I will translate to you the interesting letter, which may be condensed into one comprehensive sentence towards the end — 'When you are ready say "jump." ' "

Here Baggin appeared in the doorway, and beckoned to the polite Silinski, and that worthy made his way through the crowded room.

"Can you get that letter?" asked Baggin, without any preliminary, "or were you only joshing?"

"I can not only get the letter, but I have the letter," said the other calmly, and Baggin's lids narrowed. "Further, your plans are very foolish," the Pole went on smoothly, "because you have no plans. Spain will not hold nine defaulting bucket-shop keepers—that is the idiom, is it not?—unless your retirement is organized with considerably more skill than you have up to this moment displayed."

The American said nothing.

"I have a plan, a great plan," said Silinski, and he drew himself erect in the pride of his authorship; "but you must take me into its working."

"You are a damned villain," said Baggin, "a blackmailer——"

Silinski's brows darkened.

"Villain, yes," he said; "blackmailer, no—I am a genius—that is all."

CHAPTER III

SOME DISAPPEARANCES

In the month of March, 1904, a notice was posted
on the doors of the London, Manhattan and Jersey
Syndicate, in Moorgate Street. It was brief, but
it was to the point—

"Owing to the disappearance of Mr. George T.
Baggin, the L. M. and J. Syndicate has suspended
operations."

With Mr. Baggin had disappeared the sum of
£247,000. An examination of the books of the firm
revealed the fact that the London, Manhattan, and
Jersey Syndicate was—Mr. Baggin; that its im-
posing title thinly disguised the operations of a
bucket-shop, and the vanished bullion had been
most systematically collected in gold and foreign
notes.

Mr. Baggin had disappeared as though the earth
had swallowed him up. He was traced to Liverpool; a ticket to New York had been purchased
by a man answering to his description, and he had
embarked on the *Lucania*. The liner called at

Queenstown, and the night she left Mr. "Coleman" was missing. His clothing and trunks were found intact in his cabin, and a pathetic note addressed to the chief steward was pinned to his pillow. It said, in the extravagant language of remorse, that overwhelmed by the horror of his position, the writer had decided to leave this world for a better, and, he trusted, brighter life. It was signed "George T. Baggin." The ship was searched from stem to stern, but no trace of the unfortunate man could be discovered.

The evening newspapers flared forth with, "Tragic End of a Defaulting Banker," but Scotland Yard, ever sceptical, set on foot certain inquiries and learnt that a stranger had been seen in Queenstown after the ship sailed. A stranger who left for Dublin, and who doubled back to Heysham; who came, *via* Manchester, back to London again. In London he had vanished completely. Whether or not this was the redoubtable George T. Baggin, was a matter for conjecture.

T. B. Smith, of Scotland Yard, into whose hands the case was put, had no doubt at all. He believed that Baggin was alive. Two months after the disappearance, the firm of Woolfe, Meyers, Limited, crumbled into dust—for Louis Meyers himself failed to take his place one fine morning in the lavishly furnished board-room in King William Street. Meyers was a dealer in Premium Bonds. A stout man, scant of breath, loose-lipped, sparing pronouns. His ingenious method of trading may be summarized in a sentence. You paid your money and he took his choice. "There can be no doubt at all," said the *Daily Megaphone,* in commenting on his disappearance, "that this wretched man, face to face with exposure which was inevitable, has taken the supreme and desperate step of suicide. His overcoat, in which was a letter to the coroner, was found on one of the seats of the Thames Embankment . . . ."

Yet Scotland Yard took no trouble to find the body. Instead, it sent its most experienced detectives to watch the seaports. T. B. Smith's instructions to his watchful subordinates were marked with sardonic levity.

"You will recognize the body of the late Louis Meyers," he wrote, "from the fact that it will be smoking a big cigar and carrying a portmanteau containing £150,000's worth of French and German notes; it speaks Engish with a slight lisp."

Most artistic of all was the passing of Lucas Damant, the Company Promoter. Damant's defalcations were the heaviest, for his opportunities were greater. He dealt in millions and stole in

millions. Taking his summer holidays in Switzer-
land, Mr. Damant foolishly essayed the ascent of
the Matterhorn without a guide. His alpenstock
was picked up at the edge of a deep *crevasse*, and
(I again quote the *Megaphone*) "yet another Al-
pine disaster was added to the alarming list of
mountaineering tragedies." What time four expert guides were endeavouring to extricate the
lost man from a bottomless pit, sixteen chartered
accountants were engaged in extracting from the
chaos of his documentary remains the true position of Mr. Damant's affairs, but the sixteen accountants, had they been sixteen hundred, and the
space of time occupied in their investigations a
thousand years, would never have been able to
balance the Company Promoter's estate to the
satisfaction of all concerned, for between debit
and credit yawned an unfathomable chasm that
close on a million pounds could not have spanned.

In the course of time a fickle public forgot the
sensational disappearance of these men; in course
of time their victims died or sought admission to
the workhouse. There were spasmodic discussions
that arose in smoke-rooms and tap-rooms, and the
question as to whether they were dead or whether
they had merely bolted, was hotly debated, but
it may be truthfully said that they were forgotten;

but not by Scotland Yard, which neither forgets nor forgives.

The Official Memory sits in a big office that overlooks the Thames Embankment. It is embodied in a man who checks, day by day, hour by hour, and minute by minute, the dark happenings of the world. He is an inconsiderable person, as personalities go, for he enters no witness-box to testify against a pallid prisoner. He grants no interviews to curious newspaper reporters, he appears in no magazine as a picturesque detector of crime, but silently, earnestly, and remorselessly, he marks certain little square cards, makes grim entries in strange ledgers, consults maps, and pores over foreign newspaper reports. Sometimes he prepares a *dossier,* as a cheap-jack makes up his prize packet, with a paper from this cabinet, a photograph from that drawer, a newspaper cutting, a docketed deposition with the sprawling signature of a dying man, a finger-print card— and all these he places in a large envelope, and addresses it in a clerkly hand to Chief Inspector So-and-So, or to the "Director of Public Prosecutions." When the case is over and a dazed man sits in a cell at Wormwood Scrubbs pondering his sentence, or, as it sometimes happens, when convict masons are at work carving initials over a grave in a prison yard, the envelope comes back to the man in the office, and he sorts the contents jealously. It is nothing to him, the sum of misery they have cast, or the odour of death that permeates them. He receives them unemotionally, distributes the contents to their cabinets, pigeonholes, guard-books, and drawers, and proceeds to make up yet another *dossier*.

All things come to him; crime in all its aspects is veritably his stock-in-trade.

When George Baggin disappeared in 1904, his simple arrangement of indexing showed the connection between the passing of Lucas Damant six months later, and the obliteration of Meyers between these times. The Official Memory knew, too, what the public had no knowledge of—namely, that there had been half a dozen minor, but no less mysterious, flittings in the space of two years.

Their stories, briefly and pithily told, were inscribed on cards in the silent man's cabinet. Underneath was the significant word, "Incomplete." They were stories to be continued; some other hand than his might take up the tale at a future time, and subscribe "Finis" to their grim chapters. He was satisfied to carry the story forward as far as his information allowed him.

There never was a more fascinating office than

this of the Silent Recorder's. It was terribly busi-
nesslike with its banked files, its innumerable
drawers, its rows of deep cabinets, "A,B,C,D,"
they ran, then began all over again, "AA, BB,
CC," except the big index drawer where "Aabot,
Aaroon, Aato, Abard, Abart," commenced the
record of infamous men. There were forgers here,
murderers, coiners, defaulters, great and small
(Silinski's autobiography occupies a folder by itself). There are stories of great swindles, and of
suspected swindles, of events apparently innocent
in themselves, behind which lie unsuspected crim-
inalities.

I show you this office, the merest glimpse of it,
so that as this story progresses, and information
comes mysteriously to the hand of the chief actor,
you will understand that no miracle has been per-
formed, no heaven-sent divination of purpose has
come to him, but that at the back of the knowledge
he employs with such assurance, is this big office
at New Scotland Yard. A pleasant office overlooking the Embankment with its green trees and its
sunny river and its very pleasant sights—none of
which the Recorder ever sees, being short-sighted
from overmuch study of criminal records.

CHAPTER IV

INTRODUCING T. B. SMITH

In the month of October the market, that unfailing barometer of public nerves, moved slowly in an upward direction.

If the "House" was jubilant, the "Street" was no less gratified, for since the "Baggin Failure" and financial cataclysm which dragged down the little investors to ruin, there had been a sad flatness in the world of shares. There are many places of public resort where the "Street" people meet —those speculators who daily, year in and out, promenade the pavement of Throgmorton Street, buying and selling on an "eighth" margin.

To them from time to time come the bareheaded clerks with news of this or that rise or fall, to receive instructions gravely imparted, and as gravely accepted, and to retire to the mysterious deeps of the "House" to execute their commissions.

The market was rising steadily, as the waters of a river rise; that was the most pleasant knowledge of all. It did not jump or leap or flare; it

progressed by sixteenths, by thirty-seconds, by
sixty-fourths; but all down the money columns
in the financial papers of the press were tiny little
plus marks which brought joy to the small in-
vestor, who is by nature a "bull."

Many people who are not directly interested in
finance regarded the signs with sympathy. The
slaves of the street, 'busmen, cabmen, the sellers
of clamorous little financial papers, all these par-
took in the general cheeriness.

Slowly, slowly, climbed the market.

"Like old times," said a hurrying clerk; but the
man he spoke to sniffed contemptuously, being by
nature one of that sour class from which all bear-
dom is recruited.

"Like old times!" chuckled a man standing at
the Bodega bar, a little dazed with his prosperity.
Somebody reminded him of the other booms that
had come and undergone sudden collapse, but the
man standing at the counter twiddled the stem of
the glass in his hand and smiled indulgently.

"Industrials are the feature," said an evening
paper, and indeed the biggest figures behind the
tiny plus marks were those against the famous
commercial concerns best known in the city. The
breweries, the bakeries, the cotton corporations,
the textile manufacturing companies enjoying

quotation in the share list—all these participated in the upward rush; nay, led the van.

Into Old Broad Street on one day at the height of the boom, came a man a little above middle height, clean-shaven, his face the brick tan of one who spends much of his life in the open air. He wore a suit of blue serge, well cut but plain, a spotless grey Tirai hat, broad-brimmed, white spats over his patent shoes, and a thin cane in his hand. "A fellow in the Kaffir market" guessed one of the group about the corner of Change Alley, but somebody better informed turned hastily when he saw the quick striding figure approaching, and dived down a side court.

A showily-attired young man, standing on the edge of the pavement chewing a quill toothpick thoughtfully, did not see the newcomer until he was close on him, then started and changed colour. The man in the wide-brimmed hat recognized him and nodded. He checked his walk and stopped.

"Here's Moss," he said. He had a snappy, curt delivery and a disconcerting habit of addressing one in the third person. "How is Moss? Straight now? Straight as a die, I'll swear. He's given up rig...ag, given up Punk Prospectuses for Petty Punters. Oh, Moss! Moss!"

He shook his head with gentle melancholy,

though a light twinkled in his humorous grey eyes.

"I don't know why you're so 'ard on me, Mister Smith," said the embarrassed Moss; "we've all got our faults——"

"Not me, Mr. Moss," said T. B. Smith promptly.

"I dessay even you, sir," insisted the other. "I've 'ad my flutter; and I failed. There's lots of people who've done more than I ever done, worse things, and crookeder things, who are livin' in what I might call the odour of sanctity.

"There's people in the 'Ouse," Moss wagged an admonitory finger towards 'Change, and his tone was bitter but envious, "who've robbed by the million, an' what do we see?"

T. B. Smith shook his head.

"We see," said the indignant young man, "motor cars, an' yachts, an' racehorses—because they 'aven't been found out!"

"Moral," mused T. B. Smith, "don't allow yourself——"

"I know, I know," Moss loftily waved aside the dubious morality of Mr. Assistant-Commissioner Smith. "But I *was* found out. Twelve months in the second division. Is that justice?"

"It all depends," cautiously, "what you mean by justice. I thought the sentence was rather light."

"Look here, Mr. Smith," said Mr. Moss firmly; "let's put the matter another way round. Here's Baggin's case, an' Meyers' case. Now I ask you, man to man, are these chaps dead?"

T. B. Smith was discreetly silent.

"Are they dead?" again demanded Moss, with emotion. "You know jolly well they ain't. You know as well as I do who's at the bottom of these bear raids to send the market into the mud. I know them raids!" in his excitement Mr. Moss got further and further away from the language of his adoption; "they smell o' Baggin, George T. Baggin; he's operatin' somewhere. I recognize the touch. George T. Baggin, I tell you, an' as the good book says, his right hand hath not lost its cunnin'."

"And," said T. B. Smith, blandly ignoring the startling hypothesis; "what is Mr. Moss doing now to earn the bread, butter, and etceteras of life?"

"Me? Oh, I'm in the East mostly," said the other moodily; "got a client or two; give a tip an' get a tip now an' again. Small money an' small profits."

He dropped his eyes under the steady and pseudo-benevolent gaze of the other.

"No companies?" said the detective softly. "No companies, Mr. Moss? No Amalgamated Peruvian Concessions, eh? No Brazilian Rubber and Exploitation Syndicate?"

The young man shifted his feet uneasily.

"Genuine concerns, them," he said doggedly; "an' besides, I'm only a shareholder."

"Not promoter. Mr. Moss is not a promoter?"

In desperation the badgered shareholder turned.

"How in 'eaven's name you get hold of things I don't know," he said in helpless annoyance. "An' all I can say—excuse me."

T. B. Smith saw his expression undergo a sudden change.

"Don't look round, sir," said the other breathlessly; "there's one o' my clients comin' along; genuine business, Mr. Smith; don't crab the deal."

In his agitation he grew a little incoherent.

T. B. Smith might have walked on discreetly, leaving Moss to transact his business in quiet and peace. Indeed, the young man's light blue eyes pleaded for this indulgence; but the gentleman from Scotland Yard was singularly obtuse this morning.

"You don't want to meet him," urged Mr. Moss. "He's not in your line, sir; he's a gentleman."

"I think you're very rude, Mr. Moss," said T. B. Smith, and waited, whilst Moss and client met.

The client may have been a gentleman; he was certainly opulent. The day being fairly mild, T. B. Smith thought the client's fur-lined coat a superfluity, but the silk hat which overtopped the client's thin, long face was most correct.

"Permit me," said Moss with all the grace he could summon at a moment's notice, "to introduce you to a friend of mine—name of Smith—in the Government."

The stranger bowed and offered a gloved hand.

"Er——" said T. B., hesitant. "I did not quite catch your name."

"Count Poltavo," said Mr. Moss defiantly; "a friend of mine an' a client."

"Delighted to make your acquaintance, Count. I have met you somewhere."

The Count bowed.

"It is ver' likely. I have been in England before."

T. B. Smith with his head on one side, so ridiculously reminiscent of an inquisitive bird, surveyed the imperturbable foreigner with interest.

"But for the integrity of Mr. Moss," he said, "I should believe that I had been introduced to quite an old friend of mine—Gregory Silinski, to wit."

The foreigner smiled, showing two regular rows of white teeth.

"You think of my cousin, of whom there is some resemblance—a bad lot." He shook his head sternly and reprovingly.

"A bad lot, indeed," agreed T. B. Smith, and offered his hand to Moss.

"Good-day to you, Mr. Moss," he said; "keep out of mischief; good-bye, Mr. Silinski." He looked at his watch. "It wants four minutes to twelve; and if by five minutes to twelve tomorrow you are still in England, I shall arrest you. *Comprenez?*"

"*Parfaitement,*" said Silinski, who prided himself upon his ability to accept a situation.

T. B. Smith resumed his walk. At the corner of Threadneedle Street an able-bodied hawker offered him his choice of a box of matches or a pair of bootlaces.

"Neither in mine," said T. B. Smith. "Have you got a hawker's license, my man?"

"Yes, sir."

The hawker produced from the inside pocket

of his frowsy jacket a folded paper, and T. B. Smith examined it carefully. He must have read every word of it twice. After a while, he handed it back and what he said was not about hawkers, or licenses.

"I know they are here," he said as though referring to people whose names were inscribed on the paper he had been reading, "but they don't count, they are too small. Silinski, do you know him?"

"I've seen him," said the hawker; "wasn't he deported over the Griffon Street affair?"

T. B. Smith nodded.

"He's way along," he said, with a jerk of his head in the direction of Moss and client; "get one of your men to watch and report."

"Very good, sir."

T. B. Smith continued in the direction of the Mansion House. A famous banker passing in his motor brougham, waved his hand in salute; a city policeman stolidly ignored him.

Along Cheapside, with the deliberate air of a sightseer, the man in the grey felt hat strolled, turning over in his mind the problem of the boom.

For it was a problem.

If you see on one hand ice forming on a pool, and on the other a thermometer rising slowly to blood-heat, you may be satisfied in your mind that something is wrong somewhere. Nature cannot make mistakes. Thermometers are equally infallible. Look for the human agency at work on the mercury bulb, for the jet of hot air directed to the instrument. In this parable is explained the market position, and T. B. Smith, who dealt with huge, vague problems like markets and wars and national prosperity, was looking for the hot-air current.

The market rises because big people buy big quantities of shares; it falls because these same people sell, and T. B. Smith happened to know that nobody was buying. That is, nobody of account—Eckhardt's, Tollington's, or Bronte's Bank. You can account for the rise of a particular share by some local and favourable circumstance, but when the market as a whole moves up——?

"We can trace no transactions" wrote Mr. Louis Vell, of the firm of Vell, Vallings & Boys, Brokers, "carried out by or on behalf of the leading jobbers. The marked improvement in Industrial Stocks is due, as far as we can gather, to Continental buying—an unusual circumstance."

Who was the "philanthropist" who was making a market in stagnant stocks? Whoever it was, he or they repented long before T. B. Smith had reached the Central Criminal Court, which was his objective.

He was a witness in the Gildie Bank fraud case, and his cross-examination at the hands of one of the most relentless of counsel occupied three hours. This concluded to everybody's satisfaction, save counsel, T. B. Smith, who hated the law courts, walked out into Old Baily to find newsboys loudly proclaiming, "Slump on the Stock Exchange!"

"Thank heaven, that bubble's burst!" said T. B. piously, and walked back to Scotland Yard, whistling.

He did not doubt that the artificial rise had failed, and that the market had gone back to normal.

At the corner of the Thames Embankment he bought a paper, and the first item of news he read was:

"Consols have fallen to 84."

Now, Consols that morning had stood at 90, and T. B. Smith stopped whistling.

CHAPTER V

THE ANTICIPATORS

T. B. Smith strolled into the room of Superintendent Elk.

Elk was a detective officer chiefly remarkable for his memory. A tall, thin, sad man, who affects a low turned-down collar and the merest wisp of a black tie. If he has any other pose than his desire to be taken for a lay preacher, it is his pose of ignorance on most subjects. Elk's attitude to the world at large is comprehended in the phrase, ''I am a child in these things,'' which accounts to a very great extent for the rapidity of his promotion in the Criminal Investigation Department.

T. B.'s face wore a frown, and he twirled a paper-knife irritably.

''Elk,'' he said, without any preliminary, ''the market has gone to the devil.''

''Again?'' said Elk politely, having knowledge without interest.

''Again,'' said T. B. emphatically, ''for the

50

fourth time this year. I've just seen one of the
Stock Exchange Committee, and he's in a terrible
state of mind. Stocks and shares are nothing to
me,'' the Commissioner went on, seeing the patient boredom on the other's face, ''and I know
there is a fairly well-defined law that governs
the condition of the Stock Exchange. Prices go
see-sawing up and down, and that is part of the
day's work, but for the fourth time, and for no
apparent reason, the market is broken. Consols
are down to 84.''

''I once had some shares in an American copper mine,'' reflected Elk, ''and a disinterested
stock-jobber advised me to hold on to them; I'm
still holding, but it never occurred to me—I lost
£500—that it was a matter for police investigation.''

The Commissioner stopped in his walk and
looked at the detective.

''There's little romance in finance,'' he mused,
''but there *is* something behind all this; do you
remember the break of January 4th?''

Elk nodded; he saw there was a police side to
this slump, and grew alert and knowledgeable.

''Yankees and gilt-edged American stock came
tumbling down as though their financial founda-

tions had been dug away. What was the cause?''

Elk thought.

"Wasn't it the suicide of the President of the 11th National Bank?" he asked.

"Happened after the crash," said T. B. promptly. "Do you remember the extraordinary slump in Russian Fours in April—a slump which, like the drop in Yankees, affected every market? What was the cause?''

"The attempt on the Czar."

"Again you're wrong," said the other; "the slump anticipated the attempt, it did not follow it. Then we have the business of the 9th of August."

"The Kaffir slump?"

"Yes."

"But, surely, the reason for that may be traced," said Elk; "it followed the decision of the Cabinet to abolish coloured labour on the mines."

"It anticipated it," corrected his chief, with a twinkle in his eye, "and do you remember no other occurrence that filled the public mind about that time?"

Elk thought with knit brows.

"There was the airship disaster at the Palace. Hike Mills was put away just about then for blackmail; there was the Vermont case—and the Sud Express wreck——''

"That's it," said the Commissioner, "wrecked outside Valladolid, three killed, many injured—do you remember who was killed?"

"Yes," said Elk slowly, "a Frenchman whose name I've forgotten, Mr. Arthur Saintsbury, a King's Messenger—by George!"

The connection dawned upon him, and T. B. grinned.

"Killed whilst carrying dispatches to the King of Portugal," he said.

"Those dispatches related to the proposed withdrawal of native labour—much of which is recruited in Portuguese West Africa"; he paused a moment, and added as an afterthought, "his dispatch-box was never found."

There was silence.

"You suggest?" said Elk suddenly.

"I suggest there is an intelligent anticipator in existence who is much too intelligent to be at large." The Commissioner walked to the door.

He stood for a moment irresolutely.

"I offer you two suggestions," he said; "the first is that the method which our unknown operator is employing is not unlike the method of Mr.

George Baggin who departed this life some four years ago. The second is, that if by any chance I am correct in my first surmise, we lay this ghost for good and all."

CHAPTER VI

AT BRONTE'S BANK

It was two days later, when Consols touched 80, that T. B. Smith gathered in Elk and marched him into the City.

The agitated Committee-man of the Stock Exchange met them in his office and led them to his private room.

"I must tell you the whole story," he said, after he had carefully shut and locked the door. "Last Wednesday, the market still rising and a genuine boom in sight, Mogseys— they're the biggest firm of brokers in the city—got a wire from their Paris agents, which was to this effect: 'Sell Consols down to 80.' They were standing then at 90, and were on the up grade. Immediately following the wire, and before it could be confirmed, came another instruction in which they were told to sell some gilt-edged stocks—this was on a rising market, too—down to prices specified. I have seen the list, and taking the prices as they stood on Wed-

nesday morning and the price they stand at today,
the difference is enormous—something like three
millions."

"Which means——?"

"Which means that the unknown bears have
pocketed that amount. Well, Mogseys were para-
lyzed at the magnitude of the order, and cabled
away to their agent asking for particulars, and
were equally dumbfounded to learn that they were
acting on behalf of the Credit Bourbonaise, one
of the biggest banks in the South of France. There
was nothing else to do but to carry out the order,
and on Thursday morning they had hammered
stocks down ten points—stocks that have never
fluctuated five points each way in mortal memory!"

The Committee-man, speaking in tones of rever-
ence of these imperturbable securities, mopped
his forehead with a tumultuous bandana.

"Now," he resumed, "we know all the bears
throughout all the world. The biggest of 'em is
dead. That was George T. Baggin, one of the
most daring and unscrupulous operators we have
ever had in London. We know every man or woman or corporation likely to jump on to the market with both feet and set it snagging—but there
isn't a single known bear who has a hand in this.

We've tried to discover his identity, but we've
always come up against a blank wall—the bank.
The bank can't give away its client, and even if it
did, I doubt very much whether we should be any
the wiser, for he's pretty sure to have hidden himself too deep. We'd probably find the bank was
instructed by a broker, and the broker by another
bank, and we'd be as far off a solution as ever."

"Is there any cause for the present break?"

"I'm coming to that. In all previous slumps
there has been a very good excuse for a panic
hanging round. In the present instance no such
excuse exists. There is a good feeling abroad,
money is free and the Bank Rate is low, and the
recent spurt in Kaffirs and Yankee rails has put
a good heart into the market—why, even Bronte's
have dealt!"

He mentioned the name of the great bank,
which in the City of London, ranks only second
to the Bank of England.

"I don't know exactly the details of their dealing, but it is pretty generally known in the City
that they have increased their commitments, and
when a conservative house like Bronte's take advantage of a spell of prosperity, you may be sure
that peace is in the very air we breathe."

T. B. Smith was thoughtfully rolling a glass

paperweight up and down a blotting-pad, and Elk was regarding the ceiling with an air of pained resignation.

Neither of the two spoke when the Committee-man finished his recital, or when he looked from one to the other, secretly disappointed that two men of whom he expected so much should be so little perturbed, indeed, so little interested, by his story. He waited a little longer for them to offer some remark, and, finding that neither had any comment to make, he asked a little impatiently—

"Well?"

T. B. roused himself from his reverie, and Elk brought his gaze to earth.

"Would you mind telling me the names of the stocks again?" asked T. B., "the stocks that are being attacked."

The member recited a list.

"Um!" said the Commissioner thoughtfully. "Industrials, breweries, manufactories—the very shares that enjoyed the boom and are now undergoing the slump!

"Will you give me a Stock Exchange Year-book?"

"Certainly."

He unlocked the door and went out, re-appearing shortly with a fat brown volume.

T. B. turned the pages of the book with quick, nervous fingers, consulting the list at his side from time to time.

"Thank you," he said at length, pushing the book from him and rising.

"Have you any idea——?" the broker began, and T. B. laughed.

"You nearly said 'clue,' " he smiled; "yes, I've lots of ideas—I'm just going to work one of them out."

He bowed slightly and the two detectives left the building together.

At the corner of Threadneedle Street he bought an evening paper.

"Issued at 4:10," he said, glancing at the "fudge" space, where the result of a race had been printed, "and nothing has happened."

He hailed a passing cab and the two men got in.

"Bronte's Bank, Holborn," was the direction he gave.

"Like the immortal Mrs. Harris, there ain't no Bronte, as you know," he said. "The head of the business is Sir George Calliper. He's an austere young man of thirty-five or thereabouts. President of philosophical societies and patron of innumerable philanthropies."

"Has no vices," added Elk.

"And therefore a little inhuman," commented T. B. "Here we are."

They drew up before the severe façade of Bronte's, and dismissed the cab.

The bank was closed, but there was a side door —if, indeed, such an insignificant title could be applied to the magnificent portal of mahogany and brass—and a bell, which was answered by a uniformed porter.

"The bank is closed, gentlemen," he said when T. B. had stated his errand.

"My business is very urgent," said T. B. imperatively, and the man hesitated.

"I am afraid Sir George has left the building," he said, "but if you will give me your cards I will see."

T. B. Smith drew a card from his case. He also produced a tiny envelope, in which he inserted the card.

A few minutes later the messenger returned.

"Sir George will see you," he said, and ushered them into an anteroom. "Just a moment, gentlemen, Sir George is engaged."

Ten minutes passed before he came again. Then he reappeared, and they followed him along a marble-tiled corridor to the sanctum of the great man.

It was a large room, solidly and comfortably furnished and thickly carpeted. The only ornamentation was the beautifully carved mantel, over which hung the portrait of Septimus Bronte, who, in 1743, had founded the institution which bore his name.

Sir George Calliper rose to meet them.

He was a tall young man with sandy hair and a high, bald forehead. From his square-toed boots to his black satin cravat he was commercial solidity personified. T. B. noted the black ribbon watchguard, the heavy, dull gold signet-ring, the immaculately manicured nails, the dangling, black-rimmed monocle, and catalogued his observations for future reference. Elk, who saw with another eye and from a different point of view, mentally recorded a rosebud on the carpet and a handkerchief.

"Now, what can I do for you?" asked Sir George; he picked up the card from the desk and refreshed his memory.

"We're very sorry to trouble you," began T. B. conventionally, but the baronet waved the apology aside.

"I gather you have not come to see me out of office hours without cause," he said, and his tone rather suggested that it would be unpleasant even for an Assistant-Commissioner, if he had.

"No, but I've come to make myself a nuisance— I want to ask you questions," said T. B. coolly.

"So long as they are pertinent to the business in hand, I shall have every pleasure in answering," replied Sir George.

"First and foremost, is there the slightest danger of Bronte's Bank failing?" asked T. B. Smith calmly.

The audacity of the question struck the baronet dumb.

"Failing?" he repeated, "Bronte's fail—Mr. Smith, are you jesting?"

"I was never more in earnest," said T. B. "Think what you like of my impertinence, but humour me, please."

The banker looked hard at the man before him, as though to detect some evidence of ill-timed humour.

"It is no more possible for Bronte's to fail, than the Bank of England," he said brusquely.

"I am not very well acquainted with the practice of banking," said T. B., "and I should be grateful if you would explain why it is impossible for a bank to fail."

If Sir George Calliper had been a little less sure of himself, he would have detected the monstrous inaccuracy of T. B.'s confession of ignorance.

"But are you really in earnest?"

"I assure you," said T. B. seriously, "that I regard this matter as being one of life and death."

"Well," said the banker, with a perplexed frown, "I will explain. The solvency of a bank, as of an individual, is merely a matter of assets and liabilities. The liabilities are the elementary debts, deposits, loans, calls, and such like, that are due from the bank to its clients and shareholders. Sometimes the liability takes the form of a guarantee for the performance of certain obligations—that is clear enough?"

T. B. nodded.

"Assets may be represented as gold, Government securities and stock convertible into gold, properties, freehold, leasehold, land; but you know, of course, the exact significance of the word assets?"

T. B. nodded again.

"Well, it is a matter of balance," said the banker; "allowing a liberal margin for the fluctuation of securities, we endeavour to and succeed in keeping a balance of assets in excess of our liabilities."

"Do you keep gold in any quantity on the premises?—what would be the result, say, of a successful burglary that cleared your vaults?"

"It would be inconvenient," said Sir George, with a dry smile, "but it would not be disastrous."

"What is your greatest outstanding liability?" demanded T. B.

The banker looked at him strangely.

"It is queer that you should ask," he said slowly, "it was the subject of a discussion at my board meeting this afternoon—it is the Wady Semlik Barrage."

"The Egyptian irrigation scheme?" asked T. B. quickly.

"Yes, the bank's liability was very limited until a short time ago. There was always a danger that the physical disabilities of the Soudan would bring about a fiasco. So we farmed our liability, if you understand the phrase. But with the completion of the dam, and the report of our engineer that it had been submitted to the severest test, we curtailed the expensive insurance."

"When are the works to be handed over to the Egyptian Government?"

Sir George smiled.

"That I cannot tell you," he said, "it is a secret known only to the directors and myself."

"But until it is officially handed over, you are liable?"

"Yes, to an extent. As a matter of fact, we shall only be fully liable for one day. For there is a clause in the agreement which binds the Government to accept responsibilities for the work seven days after inspection by the works department, and the bulk of our insurances run on till within twenty-four hours of that date. I will tell you this much: the inspection has taken place, I cannot give you the date—and the fact that it was made earlier than we anticipated is responsible for the cancellation of the insurances."

"One more question, Sir George," said T. B. "Suppose, through any cause, the Wady Semlik Barrage broke on that day—the day upon which the bank was completely liable—what would be the effect on Bronte's?"

A shadow passed over the banker's face.

"That is a contingency I do not care to contemplate," he said curtly.

He glanced at his watch.

"I have not asked you to explain your mysterious visit," he said, with a smile, "and I am afraid I must curb my curiosity, for I have an appointment in ten minutes, as far west as Portland

Place. In the meantime, it may interest you to read the bank's balance-sheet.''

Elk's vacant eye was on him as he opened a drawer in his desk.

He closed it again hurriedly with a little frown. He opened another drawer and produced a printed sheet. ''Here it is,'' he said. ''Would you care to see me again at ten tomorrow?''

T. B. might have told him that for the next twelve hours the banker would hardly be out of sight for an hour, but he replied—

''I shall be very pleased.''

He had shaken hands with Sir George, and was on his way to the door, when Elk gave a sign which meant ''cover my movements,'' and T. B. turned again.

''By the way,'' he said, pointing to the picture over the fireplace, ''that is *the* Bronte, is it not?''

Sir George turned to the picture.

''Yes,'' said he, and then with a smile, ''I wonder Mr. Bronte did not fall from his frame at some of your questions.''

T. B. chuckled softly as he followed the uniformed doorkeeper along the ornate corridor.

In a cab being driven rapidly westward, Elk solemnly produced his finds.

''A little rose and a handkerchief,'' he said.

T. B. took the last-named article in his hand. It was a delicate piece of flimsiness, all lace and fragrance. Also it was damp.

"Here's romance," said T. B., folding it carefully and putting it in his pocket. "Somebody has been crying, and I'll bet it wasn't our friend the banker."

CHAPTER VII

SILINSKI EXPLAINS

T. B. Smith was dressing for dinner in his room at the Savoy, his mind occupied by speculations that centered round a mill dam, when there came a gentle tap at the door.

"Come in," he said, having all but completed his somewhat elaborate toilet—he was ever a little fastidious in the matter of personal adornment.

The door opened, and there came into his room a gentleman in evening dress, very beautiful to behold.

His shirt-front was soft and pleated, and there were three little diamond buttons to fasten it. His dress suit fitted him almost as well as the white gloves on his hands, and if the velvet collar of his coat was a little daring, he had the distinguished air of the educated and refined foreigner to carry off his sartorial extravagance.

"Come in, Silinski," said T. B., without turning round. "Twenty-four hours I gave you—when do you leave?"

"May I take a chair?"

68

Silinski was suave, polite, deferential, all the things that a well-bred man of the world should be.

"Sorry—chuck those things of mine from the chair by the bed."

So far from "chucking" anything anywhere, Silinski removed the various articles of attire one by one, folded them, and placed them in a neat pile on the bed.

Then he seated himself carefully.

"Mr. Smith," he began, "it was written by the illustrious philosopher Epictetus——"

"Do not," begged T. B., in the throes of manipulating a dress tie, "do not quote any of your disreputable friends, I beg."

"Then," said Silinski, unabashed, "let me put the matter in another way. Medical authority has it that all human-kind changes once in every seven years. New tissues replace the old, of superior or inferior quality according to age and temperament; but assuredly an entire change comes to every man."

"The last man who cited to me the born-again theory—which, by the way, is an old one in criminal circles," interrupted T. B., "is now living in retirement near Princetown because unfortunately, there was enough of the old tissue left in him to induce him to commit crimes for which, I do not doubt, the new tissue experienced the greatest shame and indignation.''

"It is foolish," reflected Silinski, clasping his knee and gazing pensively to the ceiling, "to attempt to pit one's feeble wit against a philosopher and a gentleman of your calibre. Coming down to foundations—that is your idiom, I believe—is it necessary that I should leave England?''

"It is," said T. B., confronting him now.

"Because years ago I was indiscreet,'' pursued Silinski, ''a poor waif without a friend in this vast city; hungry, alone, half mad with solitude and starvation; because in those far-off days I stole a little, is my sin to be visited on my head in the days of my affluence?''

The unsympathetic T. B. grinned.

"What a liar you are, Silinski," he said admiringly. "Friendless! starving! why, you beggar, you were living on the fat of Europe! Have you forgotten the reason for your deportation? A friend of yours threw a bomb——''

Silinski raised a protesting hand.

"There is no need to go farther," he said with dignity, "the circumstances of my persecution had for the moment escaped my memory. I must go?''

T. B. nodded. He nodded most emphatically.

"Go you must," he transposed, and Silinski rose to his feet slowly and sadly.

"You would favour me if you extended the period," he said. "I have many interests in this country which will require time to realize. Also my sister is here, with obligations of a character not to be overridden: she is not without some little fame.

He took from the breast pocket of his coat a highly-coloured picture post-card, and handed it to the detective.

"You might not know that La Belle Espagna, whose dancing at the Philharmonic has aroused the populace to enthusiasm, has the misfortune to have for brother Gregory Silinski, patriot and outcast."

He struck a little attitude, and T. B. smiled again.

"I have been aware of that fact for many months," he said, and Silinski could not control the look of astonishment and uneasiness that crossed his face.

"In fact, my dear friend," said T. B., dropping easily into French. "I know everything."

He watched carelessly for some sign of alarm in the other, and was immediately gratified. The wonder was that one of Silinski's experience should have been deceived by the bluff T. B. was making.

"Because I know of these things," continued T. B. Smith, enjoying the mystery he was creating, "I desire your absence. Let us, however, extend the period of grace to three days, at the end of which time I would have you in a land where your genius is appreciated to a greater extent than in this land of England."

Silinski stood in the centre of the room, his head bent forward, his whole attitude suggestive of feline activity, and suddenly T. B. felt the airy badinage of his own tone ring hollow, and there came to him a realization that in some indefinable way he was in deadly peril.

What secret had he surprised—what strange devilment was behind this man?

T. B. had no other regard for Silinski than as a political extremist, a mischievous egger-on of other and bolder spirits. He had never thought of Silinski as a source of danger. T. B. Smith was prompt to act.

"My man," he said evenly, "for some reason I do not like your present state of mind, and if you do monkey tricks I shall take you by the scruff of your neck and drop you out of the window."

Silinski's face was extraordinarily pale, but he did not move.

"You know—what?" he said steadily. "I am anxious, monsieur, to see where I stand. If you know what you may know, I have bungled—and if I have not, then somebody else has."

"As to my information," said T. B., "I am not prepared to extend my confidence to you. I can only warn you that you will be watched, and any attempt on your part to further certain political propaganda"—he saw a look of relief come to the other's face, and was satisfied—"will be instantly and violently suppressed."

He escorted his visitor to the lift and exchanged conventional farewells for the benefit of the lift-man, and returned slowly to his room. Then he sat down to untangle the mystery.

1. Silinski, an anarchist (*see* Dossier R.P.D., 9413, Record Department), and by his own confession.

2. Deported for inciting to murder.

3. His sister comes to London to fulfil an engagement at a first-class music-hall. ("No particular significance in this," thought T. B. "We are all liable to be cursed with unspeakable relations.")

"By the way!"

He walked across the room to where a telephone stood on the little table, and called up Elk at Scotland Yard.

"Is anything known about La Belle Espagna—the dancing girl at the Philharmonic? Yes, I know all about her brother. Eh, what's that?—people desperately in love with her? You surprise me! Who? A young lord? Elk, there is so much awe in your voice that I could not catch that last. Who is the lord? Carleby? Never heard of him. Is that all? Thanks."

He hung the receiver up.

4.   Silinski reappears, imposingly prosperous. He knows Moss, frankly, a thief.

Could they have business together, fearing detection in which, Silinski goes white? Hardly.

Then what was Silinski doing in London? Was he—a bear! T. B. had not connected the man with the bear raid. But that sort of thing was not in Silinski's line.

He sat meditating till he realized that he was hungry, and taking his overcoat from a peg behind the door, struggled into it and went out.

Elk met him at ten o'clock, and together they drove back to the Yard. There was need to dismiss Silinski from his mind.

This business of the Egyptian barrage was sufficient to occupy his thoughts.

Dimly, he began to see the workings of the gigantic combination that was spreading destruction throughout the world, anticipating disaster profitably.

Who they were he might guess; where their headquarters were situated he could not understand. In two days telegraph and cable office had been systematically ransacked for evidence upon this point. Every code, private and official, had been employed in the deciphering of messages that had arrived in London on the day of the slump and the day preceding it. The secret police of a dozen countries were acting in concert; for now that Scotland Yard had begun its investigations, many things were remembered. The Berlin financial crisis, coincided with the discovery of stolen plans, which had all but precipitated a war with Austria. Every country had its tale to tell of unaccountable depression, and their secret forces worked in unison to discover wherefore.

CHAPTER VIII

MURDER

"I've got two men on to Sir George," said T. B.
—they were at the Yard—"I've given them instructions not to leave him day or night. Now, the
question is, how will the 'bears' discover the fatal
day the barrage is to be handed over to the guile-
less Fellaheen?"

"Through the Egyptian Government?"

"That I doubt. It seems a simple proposition,
but the issues are so important that you may be
sure our mysterious friends will not strike until
they are absolutely certain. In the meantime——"

He unlocked the safe and took out a book. This,
too, was fastened by two locks. He opened it, laid
it down and began writing on a sheet of paper,
carefully, laboriously checking the result.

That night the gentleman who is responsible
for the good order of Egypt received a telegram
which ran—

"Premium Fellow Collect Wady Barrage

Meridian Tainted Inoculate Weary Sulpher.''

There was a great deal more written in the same interesting style. When the Egyptian Chief of Police unlocked his book to decode the message, he was humming a little tune that he had heard the band playing outside Shepheard's Hotel. Long before he had finished decoding the message his humming stopped.

Ten minutes later the wires were humming, and a battalion of infantry was hastily entrained from Khartoum.

Having dispatched the wire, T. B. turned to the other man, who was sitting solemnly regarding a small gossamer handkerchief and a crushed rosebud that lay on the table.

"Well," demanded T. B. Smith, leaning over the table, "what do you make of 'em?"

"They are not Sir George's," replied the cautious Elk.

"So much I gather," said T. B. "A client's?"

"A very depressed and agitated client—feel."

T. B.'s fingers touched the little handkerchief; it was still quite damp. He nodded.

"The rosebud?"

"Did you notice our austere banker's buttonhole?"

"Not particularly—but I remember no flowers."

"No," agreed Elk absently, "there were no flowers. I noticed particularly that his buttonhole was sewn and yet——"

"And yet?"

"Hidden in one of those drawers was a bunch of these roses. I saw them when he was getting your balance-sheet."

"H'm!" T. B. tapped the table impatiently.

"So you see," Elk went on, "we have an interest in this lady client of his, who comes after office hours, weeps copiously, and leaves a bunch of rosebuds as a souvenir of her visit. It may have been a client of course."

"And the roses may have been security for an overdraft," said the ironic T. B. "What do you make of the handkerchief?"

It was an exquisite little thing of the most delicate cambric. Along one hem, in letters minutely embroidered in flowing script, there ran a line of writing. T. B. took up a magnifying glass and read it.

" 'Que Dieu tu garde'," he read, "and a little monogram—a gift of some sort, I gather. As far as I can see, the lettering is 'N. H. C.'—and what that means, heaven knows! I'm afraid that beyond intruding to an unjustifiable extent into the pri-

vate affairs of our banker, we get no further. Well,
Jones?"

With a knock at the door an officer had entered.

"Sir George has returned to his house. We have
just received a telephone message from one of our
men."

"What has he been doing tonight — Sir
George?"

"He dined at home; went to his club, and returned; he does not go out again."

T. B. nodded.

"Watch the house and report," he said, and
the man saluted and left.

T. B. turned again to the contemplation of the
handkerchief.

"If I were one of those funny detectives who
live in books," he said sadly, "I could weave quite
an interesting theory from this." He held the
handkerchief to his nose and smelt it. "The scent
is 'Sympatico,' therefore the owner must have
lived in Spain, the workmanship is Parisian,
therefore——" He threw the flimsy thing from
him with a laugh. "This takes us no nearer to the
Wady Barrage, my friend—no nearer to the mysterious millionaires who 'bear' the shares of
worthy brewers. Let us go out into the open, Elk,
and ask heaven to drop a clue at our feet."

The two men turned their steps towards White-hall, and were halfway to Trafalgar Square when a panting constable overtook them.

"There is a message from the man watching Sir George Calliper's house, sir," he said; "he wants you to go there at once."

"What is wrong?" asked T. B. quickly.

"A drunken man, sir, so far as I could under-stand."

"A what?"

T. B.'s eyebrows rose, and he smiled incredu-lously.

"A drunken man," repeated the man, "he's made two attempts to see Sir George——"

"Hail that cab, Elk," said T. B. "We'll drive round and see this extraordinary person."

A drunken man is not usually a problem so difficult that it is necessary to requisition the services of an Assistant-Commissioner. This much T. B. pointed out to the detective who awaited him at the corner of St. James's Square.

"But this man is different," said the officer; "he's well-dressed; he has plenty of money—he gave the cab-driver a sovereign—and he talks."

"Nothing remarkable in that, dear lad," said T. B. reproachfully; "we all talk."

"But he talks business, sir," persisted the officer; "boasts that he's got Bronte's bank in his pocket."

"The devil he does!" T. B.'s eyebrows had a trick of rising. "Did he say anything else?"

"The second time he came," said the detective, "the butler pushed him down the steps, and that seemed to annoy him—he talked pretty freely then, called Sir George all the names he could lay his tongue to, and finished up by saying that he could ruin him."

T. B. nodded.

"And Sir George? He could not, of course, hear this unpleasant conversation? He would be out of earshot."

"Beg pardon, sir," said the plain clothes man, "but that's where you're mistaken. I distinctly saw Sir George through the half-opened door. He was standing behind his servant."

"It's a pity——" began T. B., when the detective pointed along the street in the direction of the Square.

"There he is, sir," he whispered, "he's coming again."

Along the pavement, a little unsteadily, a young man walked. In the brilliant light of a street lamp T. B. saw that he was well dressed in a glaring way. The Assistant-Commissioner waited until the newcomer reached the next lamp, then walked to meet him.

A young man, expensively garbed, red of face, and flashily jewelled—at a distance T. B. classified him as one of the more offensive type of *nouveau riche.* The stranger would have passed on his way, but T. B. stepped in front of him.

"Excuse me, Mr.——" He stopped with an incredulous gasp. "Mr. Moss!" he said wonderingly. "Mr. Lewis Moss, some time of Tokenhouse Yard, company promoter."

"Here, stash it, Mr. Smith," begged the young man. He stood unsteadily, and in his eye was defiance. "Drop all that—reformed—me. Look 'ere" —he lurched forward and caught T. B. by the lapel of his coat, and his breath was reminiscent of a distillery—"if you knew what I know, ah!"

The "Ah!" was triumph in a word.

"If you knew what I know," continued Mr. Moss with relish, "but you don't. You fellers at your game think you know *toot,* as old Silinski says; but you don't." He wagged his head wisely.

T. B. waited.

"I'm goin' to see Calliper," Mr. Moss went on, with gross familiarity, "an' what I've got to say

to him is worth millions—millions, I tell you. An'
when Calliper says to me, 'Mr. Moss, I thank you!'
and has done the right thing, I'll come to you—
see?"

"I see," said T. B.; "but you mustn't annoy Sir
George any more tonight."

"Look here, Smith," Mr. Moss went off at a
tangent, "you want to know how I got acquainted
with Silinski—well, I'll tell you. There's a feller
named Hyatt that I used to do a bit of business
with. Quiet young feller who got marvellous tips
—made a lot o' money, he did, all because he
bowled out Silinski—see?"

He stopped short, for it evidently dawned upon
him that he was talking too much.

"He sent you, eh?" Mr. Moss jerked the point
of a gold-mounted stick in the direction of Sir
George's house. "Come down off his high 'orse"
—the third "h" was too much for him—"and
very wisely, very wisely." He shook his head with
drunken gravity. "As a man of the world," he
went on, "you bein' one an' me bein' another, it
only remains to fix a meeting between self an'
client—your client—an' I can give him a few
tips."

"That," said T. B., "is precisely my desire."
He had ever the happy knack of dealing satisfac-

torily with drunken men. "Now let us review the position."

"First of all," said Mr. Moss firmly, "who are these people?" He indicated Elk and the detective. "If they're friends of yours, ole feller, say the word," and his gesture was generous, "friends of yours? Right!" Once more he became the man of affairs.

"Let us get to the bottom of the matter," said T. B. "Firstly, you wish to see Sir George Calliper?"

The young man, leaning against some happily-placed railings, nodded several times.

"Although," T. B. went on, shaking his head reprovingly, "you are not exactly——"

"A bottle of fizz—a couple, nothing to cloud the mind," said the young man airily. "I've never been drunk in me life."

"It seems to me that I have heard that remark before," said T. B., "but that's beside the matter; you were talking about a man called Hyatt who bowled Silinski."

The young man pulled himself erect.

"In a sense I was," he said with dignity, "in a sense I wasn't; and now I must be toddling."

T. B. saw the sudden suspicion that came to

him. "What do you know about the barrage?" he asked abruptly.

The man started back, sobered.

"Nothing," he said harshly. "I know nothing. I know you, though, Mr. Bloomin' Smith, and you ain't goin' to pump me. Here, I'm going."

He pushed T. B. aside. Elk would have stopped him but for a look from his chief.

"Let him go," he said. "I have a feeling that——"

The young man was crossing St. James's Street, and disappeared for a moment in the gloom between the street lamps. T. B. waited a time for him to reappear, but he did not come into sight.

"That's rum," murmured Elk, "he couldn't have gone into Sir George's; his house is on the other side of the street—hello, there he is!"

A man appeared momentarily in the rays of the lamp they were watching, and walked rapidly away.

"That isn't him," said T. B., puzzled, "he's too tall; it must be somebody from one of the houses. Let us stroll along and see what has become of Mr. Moss."

The little party crossed the street. The thoroughfare was deserted now, save for the disappearing figure of the tall gentleman.

The black patch where Moss had disappeared was the entrance of the mews.

"He must have mistaken this for a thoroughfare," said T. B. "We'll probably find him asleep in a corner somewhere." He took a little electric lamp from his pocket and shot a white beam into the darkness.

"I don't see him anywhere," he said, and walked into the mews.

"There he is!" said Elk suddenly.

The man was lying flat on his back, his eyes wide open, one arm moving feebly.

"Drunk!" said T. B., and leaned over him. Then he saw the blood and the wound in the man's throat.

"Murder! by the Lord!" he cried.

He was not dead, but even as the sound of Elk's running feet grew fainter, T. B. knew that this was a case beyond the power of the divisional surgeon. The man tried to speak, and the detective bent his head to listen. "Can't tell you all," the poor wreck whispered, "get Hyatt or the man on the Eiffel Tower—they know. His sister's got the book—Hyatt's sister—down in Falmouth—you'll find N.H.C. I don't know who they are, but you'll find them." He muttered a little incoherently, and T. B. strained his ears, but heard nothing. "N.H.

C.'' he repeated under his breath, and remembered the handkerchief.

The man on the ground spoke again—''The Admiralty—they could fix it for you.''

Then he died.

CHAPTER IX

HYATT

"Get Hyatt or the man on the Eiffel Tower!"

It sounded like the raving of a dying man, and T. B. shook his head as he walked back to his chambers in the early hours of the morning.

"Hyatt—the man on the Eiffel Tower—the Wady Barrage—the mysterious bears—what connection was there one with another?"

"To—Hyatt, a Friend of the late Lewis Moss.

"Information concerning the whereabouts of the above-mentioned Hyatt is urgently required. Immediate communication should be made to the nearest police-station."

This notice appeared under the heading, "Too late for classification" in every London newspaper the morning following the murder of Moss.

"It is possible that the name is an assumed one," said T. B., "but the Falmouth clue narrows the search."

An "all-station" message was flashed throughout the metropolis.

88

"Arrest and detain Gregory Silinski" (here followed a description), "on suspicion of being concerned in the murder of Lewis Moss."

But the surprising Silinski anticipated the arrest, for hardly had the last message been dispatched when he himself entered the portico of Scotland Yard and requested an interview with T. B.

"Yes," he said sadly, "I knew this young man. Poor fellow."

He gave a very frank account of his dealings with Moss, offered a very full explanation of his own movements on the night of the murder, threw in not a few moral sayings on the futility of life and endeavour, and was finally dismissed by a perplexed Commissioner, who detached an officer to verify all that Silinski had said.

He did not know Hyatt, confessed Silinski, had never heard the name; yet it seemed to T. B. Smith that at the mention of the mysterious Hyatt's name Silinski's lips tightened and his eyes narrowed.

T. B. was worried, and showed it after his own fashion. He sent Elk by an early train to pursue his inquiries, and then went into the City.

An interview with the head of the banking-house of Bronte was not satisfactory.

"I am satisfied," said T. B., "that an attempt will be made to destroy the barrage on the day for which you are liable. All the features of the present market position point to this fact."

"In that case," said the banker, "the 'bears' must be clairvoyant. The day on which the barrage comes into the hands of the Egyptian Government is known to two persons only. I am one, and the other is a gentleman, the mere mention of whose name will satisfy you as to his integrity."

"And none other?"

"None other," said the banker. And that was all he would say.

But at six o'clock that night T. B. received a message. It was written in pencil on the torn edges of a newspaper.

"Tonight Sir George Calliper is dining with the Spanish dancing girl, La Belle Espagna."

That, and an initial, was all the note contained, but it came from the most reliable man in the Criminal Investigation Department, and T. B. whistled his astonishment.

CHAPTER X

SIR GEORGE DINES

Sir George Calliper lived in St. James's Street. A bachelor—some regarded him as a misogynist —his establishment was nevertheless a model of order; and if you had missed the indefinable something that betrays a woman's hand in the arrangement of furniture, you recognized that the controlling spirit of the household was one possessed of a rigid sense of domesticity, that found expression in solid comfort and sober luxury.

The banker sat in his study engaged in writing a letter. He was in evening dress, and the little French clock on the mantel had just chimed seven.

He finished the note and folded it in its envelope. Then he pressed a bell. A servant entered.

"I am dining out," said Sir George shortly. "I shall be home at eleven." It was characteristic that he did not say "may be home," or "at about eleven."

"Shall I order the car, Sir George?"

"No; I'll take a cab."

A shrill whistle brought a taxi-cab to the door.

A passing commissionaire stopped to ask the cabman which was the nearest way to Berkley Square as the banker came down the two steps of the house.

"Meggioli's," he instructed the cabman, and added, "the Vine Street entrance."

The commissionaire stood back respectfully as the whining taxi jerked forward.

"Meggioli's!" murmured the commissionaire, "and by the private door! That's rum. I wonder whether Elk has started for Cornwall yet?"

He walked into St. James's Square, and a smart one-horse brougham that had been idly moving round the circle of garden in the centre, pulled up at the kerb by his side.

"Meggioli's—front entrance," said the commissionaire.

It was a uniformed man who entered the carriage; it was T. B. Smith in his well-fitting dress clothes who emerged at Meggioli's.

"I want a private room," he informed the proprietor, who came to meet him, with a bow.

"I'm ver' sorry, Mr. Smith, but I have not——"

"But you have three," said T. B. indignantly.

"I offer a thousand regrets," said the distressed

restaurateur; "they are engaged. If you had only——"

"But, name of dog! name of a sacred pipe!" expostulated T. B. unscrupulously. Was it not possible to pretend that there had been a mistake; that one room had already been engaged?

"Impossible, m'sieur! In No. 1 we have no less a person than the Premier of South-West Australia, who is being dined by his fellow-colonists; in No. 2 a family party of Lord Redlands; in No. 3—ah! in No. 3——"

"Ah, in No. 3!" repeated T. B. cunningly, and the proprietor dropped his voice to a whisper.

"La Belle Espagna!" he murmured. He named the great Spanish dancer with relish. "She, and her *fiancé's* friend, eh?"

"Her *fiancé's?*" I didn't know——"

"It is a secret——" he looked round as if he were fearful of eavesdroppers, "but it is said that La Belle Espagna is to be married to a rich admirer."

"Name?" asked T. B. carelessly.

The proprietor shrugged his shoulders.

"I do not inquire the name of my patrons," he said, "but I understand that it is to be the young Lord Carleby."

The name told T. B. nothing.

"Well," he said easily, "I will take a table in the restaurant. I do not wish to interrupt a *tête-à-tête.*"

"Oh, it is not Carleby tonight," the proprietor hastened to assure him. "I think mamzelle would prefer that it was—not; it is a stranger."

T. B. sauntered into the brilliantly lighted room, having handed his hat and coat to a waiter. He found a deserted table. Luck was with him to an extraordinary extent; that Sir George should have chosen Meggioli's was the greatest good fortune of all.

At that time Count Menshikoff was paying one of his visits to England. The master of the St. Petersburg secret police was a responsibility. For his protection it was necessary that a small army of men should be detailed, and since Meggioli's was the restaurant he favoured, at least one man of the Criminal Investigation Department was permanently employed at that establishment.

T. B. called a waiter, and the man came swiftly. He had a large white face, big unwinking black eyes, and heavy bushy eyebrows, that stamped his face as one out of the common. His name— which is unimportant—was Vellair, and foreign notabilities his specialty.

"Soup—*consommé, crème de*——"

T. B., studying his menu, asked quietly, "is it possible to see and hear what is going on in No. 3?"

"The private room?"

"Yes."

The waiter adjusted the table with a soft professional touch. "There is a small ante-room, and a ventilator, a table that might be pushed against the wall, and a chair," said the waiter, concisely. "If you remain here I will make sure."

He scribbled a mythical order on his little pad and disappeared.

He came back in five minutes with a small tureen of soup. As he emptied its contents into the plate before T. B. he said, "All right; the key is on the inside. The door is numbered 11."

T. B. picked up the wine list.

"Cover me when I leave," he said.

He had finished his soup when the waiter brought him a note. He broke open the envelope and read the contents with an expression of annoyance.

"I shall be back in a few minutes," he said rising; "reserve this table."

The waiter bowed.

CHAPTER XI

THE DANCING GIRL

T. B. reached the second floor. The corridor was deserted; he walked quickly to No. 11. The door yielded to his push. He closed it behind him and noiselessly locked it. He took a tiny electric lamp from his pocket and threw the light cautiously round.

He found the table and chair placed ready for him, and blessed Vellair silently.

The ventilator was a small one, he had located it easily enough when he had entered the room by the gleam of light that came through it. Very carefully he mounted the table, stepped lightly on to the chair, and looked down into the next chamber.

It was an ordinary kind of private dining-room. The only light came from two shaded electric lamps on the table in the centre.

Sir George with a frown was regarding his beautiful *vis-a-vis*. That she was lovely beyond ordinary loveliness T. B. knew from repute. He had expected the high colourings, the blacks and

96

scarlets of the Andalusian; but this girl had the creamy complexion of the well-bred Spaniard, with eyes that might have been hazel or violet in the uncertain light, but which were decidedly not black. Her lips, now tightly compressed, were neither too full nor too thin, her nose straight, her hair, brushed back from her forehead in an unfamiliar style, was that exact tint between bronze and brown that your connoisseur so greatly values.

A plain *filet* of dull gold about her head, and the broad collar of pearls around her neck, were the only jewels she displayed. Her dress was black, unrelieved by any touch of colour. She was talking rapidly in Spanish, a language with which T. B. was very well conversant.

"——but, Sir George," she pleaded, "it would be horrible, wicked, cruel not to see him again!"

"It would be worse if you saw him," said the other drily. "You know, my dear young lady, you would both be miserable in a month. The title would be no compensation for you; Carleby would bore you; Carleby House would drive you mad; Carleby's relatives would incite you to murder."

"You are one!" she blazed.

"Exactly; and do I not exasperate you? Think of me magnified by a hundred. Come, come, there are better men than Carleby in the world, and you are young, you are little more than a child.''

"But I love him," she sobbed.

"I suppose you do." T. B. from his hiding-place bestowed an admiring grin upon the patronage in the baronet's tone. "When did you meet him first?"

"Three weeks ago." She spoke with a catch in her voice that affected T. B. strangely.

"That girl is acting," he thought.

"Three weeks?" mused the banker. "Um—when did you discover he was a relative of mine?"

"A few days since," she said eagerly. "I was in Cornwall, visiting some friends——"

"Cornwall!" T. B. had hard work to suppress an exclamation.

"——and I learned from them that you were related. I did not know of any other relation. My friends told me it would be wicked to marry without the knowledge of his people. 'Go to Sir George Calliper and explain,' they said; 'he will help you'; instead of which——"

The banker smiled again.

"Instead of which I pointed out how impossible it was, eh? and persuaded you to give up all idea of marrying Carleby. Yes, I suppose you think I am a heartless brute.''

She sat with bent head.

"You will give him my message?" she asked suddenly.

He nodded.

"And the flowers?"

"And the flowers," he repeated gravely.

("That clears the banker," thought T. B.)

"I shall leave for Spain tomorrow. It was good of you to let me have this talk."

"It was good of you to come."

"Somehow," she said drearily. "I cannot help feeling that it is for the best."

Again T. B. thought he detected a note of insincerity.

"When will you see him?"

"Carleby?" he asked.

"Tomorrow?"

"Not tomorrow."

"The next day?"

T. B. was alert now; he saw in a flash the significance of this interview; saw the plot which had lured a foolish relative of Calliper's to a love affair; and now, the manœuvring to the crucial moment of the interview which she had so cleverly planned.

"Nor the next day," smiled Sir George.

"Well, the *next* day?"

He shook his head. "That is the day of all days I am not likely to leave London."

"Why?" she asked innocently, her eyes wide open and her lips parted.

"I have some very important business to transact on that day," he said briefly.

"Oh, I forgot," she said, with a hint of awe in her voice. "You're a great banker, aren't you?" she smiled. "Oh, yes, Carleby told me——"

"I thought you didn't know about me until your Cornish friends told you?" he asked.

"Not that you were related to him," she rejoined quickly, "but he spoke of the great house of Bronte——"

("Neat," approved the hidden T. B.)

"So Thursday will be the day," she mused.

"What day?" the banker's voice was sharp.

"The day you will see Carleby," she said, with a look of surprise.

"I said *not* Thursday on any account, but possibly the next day," said Sir George stiffly.

"She has the information she wants," said T. B. to himself, "and so have I," he reflected. "I will now retire."

He stepped carefully down, and reached the floor, and was feeling his way to the door, when a strange noise attracted his attention. It came, not from the next room, but from that in which he stood. He stood stock still, holding his breath, and the noise he heard was repeated.

Somebody was in the room with him. Somebody was moving stealthily along the wall at the opposite side of the apartment. T. B. waited for a moment to locate his man, then leaped noiselessly in the direction of the sound. His strong hands grasped a man's shoulder; another instant and his fingers were at the spy's throat. "Utter a word and I'll knock your head off!" he hissed. No terrible threat when uttered facetiously, but T. B.'s words were the reverse to humorous. Retaining a hold of his prisoner he waited until the noise of a door closing told him that the diners in the next room had departed, then he dragged his man to where he judged the electric light switch would be. His fingers found the button, turned it, and the room was instantly flooded with light.

He released the man with a little push, and stood with his back to the door.

"Now, sir," said T. B. virtuously, "will you kindly explain what you mean by spying on me?"

The man was tall and thin. He was under thirty and decently dressed; but it was his face that held the detective's attention. It was the face of a man in mortal terror—the eyes staring, the lips tremu-

lous, the cheeks lined and seamed like an old
man's. He stood blinking in the light for a moment,
and when he spoke he was incoherent and hoarse.

"You're T. B. Smith," he croaked. "I know
you; I've been wanting to find you."

"Well, you've found me," said the detective
grimly.

"I wasn't looking for you—now. I'm Hyatt."

He said this simply enough, and it was the detective's turn to stare.

"I'm Hyatt," the man went on; "and I've a
communication to make; King's evidence; but
you've got to hide me!" He came forward and
laid his hand on the other's arm. "I'm not going
to be done in like Moss; it's your responsibility,
and you'll be blamed if anything happens to me,"
he almost whispered, in his fear. "They've had
Moss, and they'll try to have me. They've played
me false because they thought I'd get to know
the day the barrage was to be handed over, and
spoil their market. They brought me up to London, because I'd have found out if I'd been in
Cornwall——"

"Steady, steady!" T. B. checked the man. He
was talking at express rate, and between terror
and wrath was well nigh incomprehensible. "Now,
begin at the beginning. Who are 'they'?"

"N. H. C., I told you," snarled the other impatiently. "I knew they were going to get the date from the banker. That was Catherine's scheme; she got introduced to his nephew so that she might get at the uncle. But I'm giving King's evidence. I shall get off, shan't I?"

His anxiety was pitiable.

T. B. thought quickly. Here were two ends to the mystery; which was the most important? He decided. This man would keep; the urgent business was to prevent Catherine from communicating her news to her friends.

"Take this card," he said, and scribbled a few words hastily upon a visiting-card; "that will admit you to my rooms at the Savoy. Make yourself comfortable until I return.

He gave the man a few directions, piloted him from the restaurant, saw him enter a cab, then turned his steps towards Baker Street.

CHAPTER XII

"MARY BROWN"

Pentonby Mansions are within a stone's throw of Baker Street Station. T. B. jumped out of his cab some distance from the great entrance hall, and paid the driver. Just before he turned into the vestibule a man strolling toward him asked him for a match.

"Well?"

"She came straight from the restaurant and has been inside ten minutes," reported the man ostentatiously lighting his pipe.

"She hasn't sent a telegram?"

"So far as I know, no, sir."

In the vestibule a hall porter sat reading the evening paper.

"Can I telephone from here?" asked T. B.

"Yes, sir," said the man, and T. B.'s heart sank, for he had overlooked this possibility.

"I suppose you have 'phones in every room?" he asked carelessly.

But the man shook his head.

"No, sir," he said; "there is some talk of putting 'em in, but so far this 'phone in my office is the only one in the building."

T. B. smiled genially.

"And I suppose," he said, "that you're bothered day and night with calls from tenants?" He waited anxiously for the answer.

"Sometimes I am, and sometimes I go a whole day without calls. No; today, for instance, I haven't had a message since five o'clock."

T. B. murmured polite surprise and began his ascent of the stairs. So far, so good. His business was to prevent the girl communicating with her brother, whom he did not doubt now was the agent of the "bears," if not worse.

He had already formed a plan in his mind.

Turning at the first landing, he walked briskly along the corridor to the left.

"29, 31, 33," he counted, "35, 37. Here we are." The corridor was empty; he slipped his skeleton key from his pocket, deftly manipulated it.

The door opened noiselessly. He was in a dark little hall-way. At the end was a door and a gleam of light shone under it. He closed the door behind him, stepped softly along the carpeted floor, and his hand was on the handle of the further door, when a sweet voice called him by name from the room.

"*Adelante! Senor Smit,*" it said; and, obeying the summons, T. B. entered.

The room was well, if floridly, furnished; but T. B. had no eyes save for the graceful figure lounging in a big wicker chair, a thin cigarette between her red lips, and her hands carelessly folded on her lap.

"Come in," she repeated. "I have been expecting you."

T. B. bowed slightly.

"Gregory told me that I should probably receive a visit from you."

"First," said T. B. gently, "let me relieve you of that ugly toy."

Before she could realize what was happening, two strong hands seized her wrists and lifted them. Then one hand clasped her two, and a tiny pistol that lay in her lap was in the detective's possession.

*   *   *   *

"Let us talk," said T. B. He laid her tiny pistol on the table, and with his thumb raised the safety catch.

"You are not afraid of a toy pistol?" she scoffed.

"I am afraid of anything that carries a nickel bullet," he confessed, without shame. "I know by experience that your 'toy' throws a shot that penetrates an inch of pinewood and comes out on the other side. I cannot offer the same resistance as pinewood," he added modestly.

"I have been warned about you," she said, with a faint smile.

"So you were warned." T. B. was mildly amused and just a trifle annoyed. It piqued him to know that whilst, as he thought, he had been working in the shadow, he had been under a searchlight.

"Your excellent brother, I do not doubt," he said.

"You are—what do you call it in England?—smug," she said, "but what are you going to do with me?"

She had let fall her cloak and was again leaning back lazily in the big armchair. The question was put in the most matter-of-fact tones.

"That, you shall see," said T. B. cheerfully. "I am mainly concerned now in preventing you from communicating with brother Gregory."

"It will be rather difficult?" she challenged with a smile. "I am not proscribed; my character does not admit——"

"As to your character," said T. B. magnanimously, "we will not go into the question. So far
as you are concerned, I shall take you into custody
on a charge of obtaining property by false pre-
tences," said T. B. calmly.

"What?"

"Your name is Mary Brown, and I shall charge
you with having obtained the sum of £350 by a
trick from a West Indian gentleman at Barbadoes
last March."

She sprang to her feet, her eyes blazing.

"You know that is false and ridiculous," she
said steadily. "What is the meaning of it?"

T. B. shrugged his shoulders.

"Would you prefer that I should charge La
Belle Espagna with being an accessory to murder?" he asked, with a lift of his eyebrows.

"You could not prove it!" she challenged.

"Of that I am aware," he said. "I have taken
the trouble to trace your movements. When these
murders were committed you were fulfilling an
engagement at the "Philharmonic," but you knew
of the murder, I'll swear—you are an agent of
N. H. C."

"So it was you who found my handkerchief?"

"No; a discerning friend of mine is entitled to

the discovery—are you ready, Mary Brown?"

"Wait."

She stood plucking at her dress nervously. "What good can my arrest do to you—tomorrow it will be known all over the world."

"There," said T. B., "you are mistaken."

"To arrest me is to sign your death-warrant— you must know that — the Nine Men will strike——"

"Ah!!"

T. B.'s eyes were dancing with excitement.

"Nine men!" he repeated slowly, *"Neuf hommes*—N. H. What does the 'C' stand for?"

"That much you will doubtless discover," she said coldly, "but they will strike surely and effectively."

The detective had regained his composure.

"I'm a bit of a striker myself," he said in English.

CHAPTER XIII

DEPORTATION

T. B. found the Chief Commissioner of Police at his club, and unfolded his plan.

The Chief looked grave.

"It might very easily lead to a horrible catastrophe if you carry that scheme into execution."

"It might very easily lead to a worse if I don't," said T. B. brutally, "I am too young to die. At the worst it can only be a 'police blunder,' such as you read about in every evening newspaper that's published," he urged, "and I look at the other side of the picture. If this woman communicates with her principals, nothing is more certain than that Thursday will see the blowing up of the Wady Semlik Barrage. These 'Nine Bears' are operating on the sure knowledge that Bronte's Bank is going to break. The stocks they are attacking are companies banking with Bronte, and it's ten chances to one they will kill Sir George Calliper in order to give an artistic finish to the failure."

110

The Commissioner bit his lip thoughtfully. "And," urged T. B. Smith, "the N. H. C. will be warned, and bang goes our only chance of bagging the lot!"

The Commissioner smiled.

"Your language, T. B.!" he deplored; then, "do as you wish—but what about the real Mary Brown?"

"Oh, she can be sent on next week with apologies. We can get a new warrant if necessary."

"Where is she?"

"At Bow Street."

"No; I mean the Spanish lady?"

T. B. grinned.

"She's locked up in your office, sir," he said cheerfully.

The Commissioner said nothing, but T. B. declined to meet his eye.

At four o'clock the next morning, a woman attendant woke La Belle Espagna from a fitful sleep, and a few minutes afterwards T. B., dressed for a journey and accompanied by a hard-faced wardress and a detective, came in.

"Where are you going to take me?" she demanded; but T. B.'s reply was not very informing.

A closed carriage deposited them at Euston in time to catch the early morning train.

In the compartment reserved for her and the wardress—it was a corridor carriage, and T. B. and his man occupied the next compartment—she found a dainty breakfast waiting for her, and a supply of literature. She slept the greater part of the journey and woke at the jolting of a shunting engine being attached to the carriage.

"Where are we?" she asked.

"We're there," was the cryptic reply of the woman attendant.

She was soon to discover, for when the carriage finally came to a standstill and the door was opened, she stepped down on to a wind-swept quay. Ahead of her the great white hull of a steamer rose, and before she could realize the situation she had been hurried up the sloping gangway on to the deck.

Evidently T. B.'s night had been profitably spent, for he was expected. The purser met him.

"We got your telegrams," he said. "Is this the lady?"

T. B. nodded.

The purser led the way down the spacious companion.

"I have prepared 'C' suite," he said, and ushered the party into a beautifully appointed cabin.

She noticed that a steel grating had been newly

fixed to the porthole, but that was the only indication of her captivity.

"I have enlisted the help of the stewardess," said T. B., "and you will find all the clothing you are likely to require for the voyage. I am also instructed to hand you three hundred pounds. You will find your little library well stocked. I, myself," he stated with all the extravagance to which the Iberian tongue lends itself, "have denuded my own poor stock of Spanish and French novels in order that you might not be dull."

"I understand that I am to be deported?" she said.

"That is an excellent understanding," he replied.

"By what authority?" she demanded. "It is necessary to obtain an order from the Court."

"For the next fourteen days, and until this ship reaches Jamaica, you will be Mary Brown, who was formally extradited last Saturday on a charge of fraud," said T. B. "If you are wise, you will give no trouble, and nobody on board need have an inkling that you are a prisoner. You can enjoy the voyage, and at the end——"

"At the end?" she asked, seeing that he paused.

"At the end we shall discover our mistake," said T. B., "and you may return."

"I will summon the captain and demand to be put ashore!" she cried.

"A very natural request on the part of a prisoner," said T. B. meditatively, "but I doubt very much whether it would have any effect upon an unimaginative seaman."

He left her raging.

For the rest of the day he idled about the ship. The *Port Sybil* was due to leave at four o'clock, and when the first warning bell had sounded he went below to take his leave.

He found her much calmer.

"I would like to ask one question," she said. "It is not like the police to provide me with money, and to reserve such a cabin as this for my use—who is behind this?"

"I wondered whether you would ask that," said T. B. "Sir George was very generous——"

"Sir George Calliper!" she gasped. "You have not dared——"

"Yes, it needed some daring," admitted T. B., "to wake an eminent banker out of his beauty sleep to relate such a story as I had to tell—but he was very nice about it."

She brooded for some moments.

"You will be sorry for this," she said. "The

Nine Men will know much sooner than you imagine.''

"Before they know this, they will know other
things,'' he said. And with this cryptic utterance
he left her.

He stood watching the great steamer moving
slowly down the Mersey. He had left the wardress
on board to make the voyage, and the other detective had remained to report.

As the vessel swung round a bend of the Mersey
out of sight, he murmured flippantly:

"Next stop—Jamaica!''

* * * *

T. B. reached his chambers at noon that day.
He stopped to ask a question of the porter.

"Yes, sir,'' said that worthy, "he arrived all
right with your card last night. I made him comfortable for the night, got him some supper, and
told my mate who is on duty at night to look after
him.''

T. B. nodded. Declining the lift-boy's services,
he mounted the marble stairs.

He reached the door of his flat and inserted the
key.

"Now for Mr. Hyatt,'' he thought, and opened
the door.

There was a little hall-way to his chambers, in

which the electric light still burned, in spite of the flood of sunlight that came from a long window at the end.

"Extravagant beggar!" muttered T. B.

The dining-room was empty, and the blinds were drawn, and here, too, the electric light was full on. There was a spare bedroom to the left, and to this T. B. made his way.

He threw open the door.

"Hyatt!" he called; but there was no answer, and he entered.

Hyatt lay on the bed, fully dressed. The handle of a knife protruded from his breast, and T. B., who understood these things, knew that the man had been dead for many hours.

CHAPTER XIV

WHEN THE MARKET ROSE

Consols were up.

There was no doubt whatever about that fact, and the industrial market was a humming hive of industry.

Breweries, bakeries, and candlestick makeries —their shares bounded joyously as though a spirit, as of early spring had entered into these inanimate and soulless things.

The mysterious "bears" were buying, buying, buying.

Frantically, recklessly buying.

Whatever coup had been contemplated by the Nine Men had failed, and their agents and brokers were working at fever heat to cover their losses.

It is significant that on the morning the boom started, there appeared in all the early editions of the evening newspapers one little paragraph. It appeared in the "late news" space and was condensed:

117

"Wady Barrage was handed over to Egyptian Government early this morning in presence of Minister of Works. Overnight rumours were prevalent that attempt made to destroy section dam by dynamite and that Italian named Soccori shot dead by sentry of West Kent Regiment in act of placing explosives on works. No official confirmation."

Interesting enough, but hardly to be associated by the crowd which thronged the approaches of the House with the rising market.

All day long the excitement in the City continued, all day long bare-headed clerks ran aimlessly—to all appearances—from 'Change to pavement, from pavement to 'Change, like so many agitated ants.

Sir George Calliper, sitting alone in the magnificence of his private office, watched the "boom" thoughtfully, and wondered exactly what would have happened if "an Italian named Soccori" had succeeded in placing his explosive.

The echoes of the boom came to T. B. Smith in his little room overlooking the Thames Embankment, but brought him little satisfaction. The Nine Men had failed this time. Would they fail on the next occasion?

Who they were he could guess. From what centre they operated, he neither knew nor guessed. For T. B. they had taken on a new aspect. Hitherto they had been regarded merely as a band of dangerous and clever swindlers, Napoleonic in their method; now, they were murderers—dangerous, devilish men, without pity or remorse.

The man Moss by some accident had been associated with them—a tool perhaps, but a tool who had surprised their secret. He was not the type of man who, of his own intelligence, would have made discoveries. He mentioned Hyatt and "the man on the Eiffel Tower." That might have been the wanderings of a dying man, but Hyatt had come to light.

Hyatt, with his curiously intellectual face; here, thought T. B., was the man, if any, who had unearthed the secret of the Nine.

Likely enough he shared confidence with Moss; indeed, there was already evidence in T. B.'s hands that the two men had business dealings. And the third—"the man on the Eiffel Tower"? Here T. B. came against a wall of improbability. His report to the Chief Commissioner deserves quotation on the point.

"Hyatt occupied rooms in Albany Street," he wrote. "So far as we have been able to ascertain, he paid rare visits to London. His landlady thought he came from the South of England, but could give me no reason for this supposition. He paid £2 a week for his chambers, and although, as I say, he was seldom in London, he kept these rooms on, which leads to the assumption that he was a man of some means. The only documents we found in our search were two penny memorandum books, filled with notes regarding share transactions. Hyatt seems to have speculated very heavily and very successfully, and it is significant that he participated in all the big 'Nine Men' operations.

"I found a bag with two hotel labels half obliterated. One of these is unquestionably the label of the Hotel de Calais in the Rue de Capucines, and the other is the representation of a white ensign. Comparing this with the hotel labels indexed on the Record Department at Scotland Yard, I am led to the belief that it was affixed at the Grand Hotel, Gibraltar. It is a fact, as you know, that amongst the possessions of Moss we discovered a hand-bag with a Paris label, but in these two bags there is a more important clue. There is affixed to both a 'Repository' label—that is, the label of a French cloak-room.

"In the case of Moss the number of the ticket

is '01795,' on Hyatt's bag there is still discernible '—796.' From this we know that not only were the two men in Paris at the same time, but that they arrived by the same train, and going together to the depository, left their bags—which were numbered consecutively.

"I am now, therefore, inclined to take a more serious view of the statement made by Moss before he died. His words were, you remember—

" 'Get Hyatt or the man on the Eiffel Tower. His sister's got the book—Hyatt's sister down in Falmouth.'

"Then he went on to say that 'the Admiralty would fix it for you.'

"At the time I thought the poor chap was raving; but Hyatt is a fact, and we are now searching for his sister and this 'book' of his. As to the reference to the Admiralty I confess I am stumped, for nobody at Whitehall has ever heard of Hyatt.

"There remains the man on the Eiffel Tower. Who was he, or is he? A theory advanced by Elk is that he is a man casually met; some acquaintance made in the course of a morning's sight-seeing. If this is so, the business of discovering his identity promises to be an extremely difficult one. We have communicated with Lepine in Paris, but naturally the little man wants something more tangible, more definite than the description we have been able to give him . . . In the meantime I have had Hyatt's body removed, and so far nothing has got into the papers about that murder. We must issue a statement tonight, if the fact does not leak out before. By the way, Silinski, the man I referred to in my minute of the 10th, was under observation at the time of the murder, and the detective engaged in shadowing him informs me that it is impossible that he could have been implicated.''

CHAPTER XV

IN THE "JOURNAL" OFFICE

The room was a long one, full of dazzling islands of light where shaded lamps above the isolated sub-editors' desks threw their white circles. This room, too, was smirched with black shadows; there were odd corners where light never came. It never shone upon the big bookcase over the mantelpiece, or in the corner behind the man who conned the foreign exchanges, or on the nest of pigeon holes over against the chief "sub."

When he would refer to these he must needs emerge blinking from the blinding light in which he worked and go groping in the darkness for the needed memorandum.

He was sitting at his desk now, intent upon his work.

At his elbow stood a pad, on which he wrote from time to time.

Seemingly his task was an aimless one. He wrote nothing save the neat jottings upon his pad. Bundles of manuscript came to him, blue books, cut-

tings from other newspapers; these he looked at
rather than read, looked at them in a hard,
strained fashion, put them in this basket or that,
as the fancy seized him, chose another bundle,
stared at it, fluttered the leaves rapidly and so
continued. He had the appearance of a man solv-
ing some puzzle, piecing together intricate parts to
make one comprehensive whole. When he hesitated, as he sometimes did, and seemed momentarily doubtful as to which basket a manuscript
should be consigned, you felt the suggestion of
mystery with which his movements were envel-
oped, and held your breath. When he had decided
upon the basket, you hoped for the best, but wondered vaguely what would have happened if he
had chosen the other.

Once he leaned back and dived into the darkness.
When he came back to light his hand held a little
book, carefully indexed and filled with written
notes.

He glanced dubiously at a bundle of copy before
him, opened the book at "E," ran his finger down
the page, turned the page over, made another
search, and frowned.

Elling was there: George Elling, who sold the
Journal a story about a suicide that had never
happened. He had derived a fairly comfortable

and regular income from reporting mythical happenings till the *Journal* sent a special man to investigate. Then the fraud was detected and "our own correspondent" at Gravesport was "fired," and his name and the record of his infamy entered in the little book with the green covers. Edwards was there too. Edwards had written a little pamphlet attacking "The Office"—a vulgarly abusive, hysterical, foolish, and illogical little pamphlet, in which personal grievances and incoherent appeals to the sanity of the country were hopelessly interwoven. Essard was there, on the second page of the "E's." No crime stood against his name, but the chief sub. smiled faintly as he passed the name, for Essard had once dared to contribute a paragraph with a "business end." In other words, the wretched Essard had had the temerity to write under the guise of a news-story, the most barefaced advertisement of a firm of engineers, thereby wickedly, maliciously, and feloniously attempting to deprive the directors and shareholders of the Amalgamated Newspapers, Limited, of their just and proper revenue.

But the sub-editor sought in vain for the name of the man under review. He closed the book and looked across the table to his assistant.

"Who is Escoltier?" he asked.

The assistant looked up.

"Escoltier? Never heard of the gentleman. What has he done?"

"Is he barred?"

"Barred—Escoltier?" This was a serious question and not to be treated with flippancy. "No, I can't remember Escoltier—rum name—being barred; in fact, I can't remember Escoltier."

The chief sub. stared at the manuscript on the desk before him.

He shook his head; hesitated, then dropped it into basket three.

The door that opened into the tape-room was swinging constantly now, for it wanted twenty minutes to eleven. Five tickers chattered incessantly, and there was a constant procession of agency boys and telegraph messengers passing in and out the vestibule of the silent building. And the pneumatic tubes that ran from the front hall to the subs'. room hissed and exploded periodically, and little leathern carriers rattled into the wire basket at the chief sub's elbow.

News! news! news!

A timber fire at Rotherhithe; the sudden rise in Consols; the Sultan of Turkey grants an amnesty to political offenders; a man kills his wife at Wolverhampton; a woman cyclist run down by a

motor-car; the Bishop of Elford denounces Non-
conformists——

News for tomorrow's breakfast table; intellectual stimulant for the weary people who are even
now kicking off their shoes with a sleepy yawn
and wondering whether there will be anything in
the paper tomorrow.

News to be carried by fast expresses north, east,
south, and west. The history of the world for one
day, told by eye-witnesses, recorded by expert reporters, telegraphed, telephoned, mailed, and written in the office at first hand.

A boy came flying through the swing door of
the tape-room, carrying in his hand a slip of
paper.

He laid it before the chief sub.

That restless man looked at it, then looked at
the clock.

"Take it to Mr. Greene," he said shortly, and
reached for the speaking-tube that connected him
with the printer.

"There will be a three-column splash on page
five," he said, in a matter-of-fact voice.

"What's up?" His startled assistant was on his
feet.

"A man found murdered in T. B. Smith's chambers," he said.

The inquest was over, the stuffy little court discharged its morbid public, jurymen gathered in little knots on the pavement permitted themselves to theorize, feeling, perhaps, that the official verdict of "murder against some person or persons unknown," needed amplification.

"My own opinion is," said the stout foreman, "that nobody could have done it, except somebody who could have got into his chambers unknown."

"That's my opinion, too," said another juryman.

"I should have liked to add a rider," the foreman went on, "something like this: 'We call the coroner's attention to the number of undiscovered murders nowadays, and severly censure the police,' but he wouldn't have it."

"They 'ang together," said a gloomy little man; "p'lice and coroners and doctors, they 'ang together, there's corruption somewhere. I've always said it."

"Here's a feller murdered," the foreman went on, "in a detective's room, the same detective that's in charge of the Moss murder. We're told his name's Hyatt, we're told he was sent to that room by the detective whilst he's engaged in some fanciful business in the north—is that sense?"

"Then there's the *Journal*," interrupted the man of gloom, "it comes out this mornin' with a cock an' bull story about these two murders being connected with the slump—why, there ain't any slump! The market went up the very day this chap Hyatt was discovered."

"Sensation," said the foreman, waving deprecating hands, "newspaper sensation. Any lie to sell the newspapers, that's their motto."

The conversation ended abruptly, as T. B. Smith appeared at the entrance to the court. His face was impassive, his attire, as usual, immaculate, but those who knew him best detected signs of worry.

"For heaven's sake," he said to a young man who approached him, "don't talk to me now— you beggar, your wretched rag has upset all my plans."

"But, Mr. Smith," pleaded the reporter, "what we said was true, wasn't it?"

"A lie that is half the truth," quoted T. B. solemnly.

"But it is true—there is some connection between the murders and the slump, and, I say, do your people know anything about the dancing girl from the Philharmonic?"

"Oh, child of sin!" T. B. shook his head reprovingly. "Oh, collector of romance!"

"One last question," said the reporter. "Do you know a man named Escoltier?"

"Not," said T. B. flippantly, "from a crow—why? Is he suspected of abducting your dancing lady?"

"No," said the reporter, "he's suspected of pulling our editor's leg."

T. B. was all this time walking away from the Court, and the reporter kept step with him.

"And what is the nature of his hoax?" demanded T. B.

He was not anxious for information, but be was very desirous of talking about nothing—it had been a trying day for him.

"Oh, the usual thing; wants to tell us the greatest crime that ever happened—a great London crime that the police have not discovered."

"Dear me!" said T. B. politely, "wants payment in advance?"

"No, that's the curious thing about it," said the reporter. "All he wants is protection."

T. B. stopped dead and faced the young man. He dropped the air of boredom right away.

"Protection?" he said quickly, "from whom?"

"That is just what he doesn't say—in fact, he's

rather vague on that point—why don't you go up and see Delawn, the editor?"

T. B. thought a moment.

"Yes," he nodded. "That is an idea. For the moment, however, I have engaged myself to meet another gentleman who may throw a light upon many matters which are at present obscure."

CHAPTER XVI

SILINSKI IS INTERVIEWED

There was no apparent connection between Homborgstrasse 22, Berlin, and No. 14, Rue de Cent, Paris, nor between the big, barren-looking house in the Calle de Recoletos in Madrid and 375, St. John Street, W. C. Nor, for the matter of that, between the little house perched upon one of the seven hills overlooking the Tagus and the pension near Novski Prospekt in Petersburg.

One feature they had in common, and that was a stout flagstaff, upon which on festal days fluttered the flag of the respective nations.

Silinski, who was responsible, for the hiring or purchasing of all these properties, could have told you another connection less apparent, but Silinski was a notoriously silent man, and said little or nothing.

He sat in his well-furnished study in St. John Street, and round him and about was evidence of his refinement and taste. Rare prints hung on the wall, the furniture was sombrely magnificent, the carpet beneath his feet soft and thick and of sober hue, the desk before him such an one as a successful man of letters might affect.

There were photographs of eminent personages, kings, statesmen, ambassadors, great prima donnas. Some of these were autographed *"a cher Silinski"*; some were framed in silver, and, in the case of royalties, surmounted by tiny gilt crowns.

Silinski had never met royalty in his life, though he had once robbed a grand duke at Monte Carlo, and the autographs and loving messages written upon the purchased photographs were in Silinski's own hand, though this fact was not generally known. This was Silinski's weakness; many a greater man has shared it.

There came a gentle tap at his door and a man entered.

"Well?" demanded Silinski suavely.

"The police, illustrious," said the man in Spanish, and with no particular sign of agitation.

Silinski nodded gravely.

"Admit," he said, and in a few seconds T. B. Smith walked into the room.

"And what is your pleasure, gentlemen?" demanded Silinski.

"Little enough, Silinski," said the other blandly. He looked round as though seeking a comfortable chair. In reality he was taking a rapid survey of the apartment. "I have a few questions to ask you."

Silinski bowed, and motioned the Assistant-Commissioner to a seat.

"It is my misfortune," he said, leaning back in his chair and crossing his legs, "that I have incurred your enmity; none the less, it will give me the greatest pleasure to afford you such assistance as lies in my power."

T. B. smiled grimly.

"You have incurred nobody's enmity, as I understand the situation," he said. He looked again round the room. "You are very comfortably circumstanced, Silinski."

"Fortune has been kind," said the Pole suavely.

"One successful speculation," mused T. B. aloud, "might found the fortunes of such a man as you."

"I am no speculator," said the other hastily. "It is too risky—I do not approve of gambling."

"Yet you had dealings with Moss?"

"Investments, m'sieur—not speculations."

"And with Hyatt?"

"As to Hyatt—I do not know him. I have never heard of him."

"And the man," T. B. paused, "from the—er—Eiffel Tower?"

Perhaps Silinski's face grew a shade whiter, and the lines about his mouth hardened.

"These riddles you set me are beyond my understanding," he said harshly. In a moment, however, he had recovered his equanimity.

"You are much too clever for me, Mr. Smith," he said, with a smile.

"There is a fourth person who would seem to be in some way associated with your complicated financial affairs," T. B. resumed. "Do you know a Monsieur Escoltier?"

Silinski sprang to his feet.

"Fourth person—M'sieur Escoltier?" he stammered. "What do you mean? I tell you, you are speaking in riddles. I do not understand you—I do not wish to understand you." His voice grew louder and louder as he spoke. His energy seemed out of all proportion to the importance of the topic, and T. B. knit his brows in perplexity.

Then he suddenly sprang to his feet.

"Stop!" he said, "stop talking! You are bellowing because something is happening in this house that you do not wish me to hear—stop!"

But the frenzy of the Pole rose. He roared indignant, unintelligible protestations; he shouted denunciations of police espionage.

T. B., with bent head and every sense alert, stood before him. Through the flood of impassioned words he detected the sound; it was a noise strangely like the rattling of dried peas in a tin can.

Then as suddenly as he began, Silinski ceased, and the two men faced one another in silence.

"Silinski," said T. B. at last, "before God, I believe you are a wicked murderer."

"Then arrest me," challenged the man; "call in the police who have been watching this house day and night since the death of Moss. Arrest me, as you did my sister!"

T. B. had all his work to suppress the exclamation of surprise that came to his lips.

"Extradite me under a false name, as you did her," sneered Silinski; "carry me up to Liverpool in the dead of night and smuggle me on board a West Indian steamer."

"I am not as a rule a curious man," said T. B. slowly, "but I must confess that I should like to know where you secured all these valuable data."

"Pooh!"

It was the old Silinski who paced the floor and

snapped his fingers—the Silinski assured, arrogant, the hint of a swagger in his walk.

"You think, you English police, that the world goes blind at your command. My friend"—he stopped and pointed a lean forefinger at the other —"I can tell you many things. The hour you left London, the hour you arrived, the number of the state-room in which you placed my poor, ill-used sister; your very words to her at parting."

He stopped, biting his lips; he had said too much, and he knew it. In the enjoyment of puzzling an astute member of a profession regarded by him as made up of his natural enemies, he had allowed boastfulness to outrun discretion.

"So you know my last words to her," repeated T. B., more slowly than ever, "although she and I were alone, although a thousand miles of sea separate you at this moment. I see."

He said no more, but with a slight nod, and without any further talk, he descended the stairs that led to the big entrance-hall, and Silinski, pulling nervously at his moustache, heard the great door of the house close behind him.

CHAPTER XVII

THE MAN FROM THE EIFFEL TOWER

In the holy of holies, the inner room within the inner room, wherein the editor of the *London Morning Journal* saw those visitors who were privileged to pass the outer portal, T. B. Smith sat, a sorely puzzled man, a scrap of disfigured paper in his hands.

He read it again and looked up at the editor.

"This might, of course, be a fake," he said.

"It doesn't read like a fake," said the other.

"Admitting your authority on the subject of fakes, Tom," said T. B.,—they were members of the same club, which fact in itself is a license for rudeness—"I am still in the dark. Why does this —what is his name?"

"Escoltier."

"Why does this man Escoltier write to a newspaper, instead of coming straight to the police?"

"Because he is a Frenchman, I should imagine," said the editor. "The French have the newspaper instinct more highly developed than the English."

T. B. looked at his watch.

"Will he come, do you think?"

"I have wired to him," said the editor.

T. B. read the paper again. It was written in execrable English, but its purport was clear.

The writer could solve the mystery of Hyatt's death, and, for the matter of that, of the Moss murder.

T. B. read it and shook his head.

"This sort of thing is fairly common," he said; "there never was a bad murder yet, but what the Yard received solutions by the score."

A little bell tinkled on the editor's desk, and he took up the receiver of the telephone.

"Yes?" he said, and listened. Then, "Send him up."

"Is it——?"

"M. Escoltier," said the editor.

A few seconds later the door was opened, and a man was ushered into the room. Short and thick-set, with a two days' growth of beard on his chin, his nationality was apparent long before he spoke in the argot of the lowly-born Parisian.

His face was haggard, his eyes heavy from lack of sleep, and the hand that strayed to his mouth shook tremulously.

"I have to tell you," he began, "about M'sieur

Moss and M'sieur Hyatt." His voice was thick, and as he spoke he glanced from side to side as though fearful of observation. There was something in his actions that vividly reminded the detective of his interview with Hyatt. "You understand," the man went on incoherently, "that I had long suspected N. H. C.—it was always so unintelligible. There was no such station and——"

"You must calm yourself, monsieur," said T. B., speaking in French; "begin at the beginning, for as yet my friend and myself are entirely in the dark. What is N. H. C., and what does it mean?" It was some time before the man could be brought to a condition of coherence. The editor pushed him gently to the settee that ran the length of the bay window of his office.

"Wait," said the journalist, and unlocking a drawer, he produced a silver flask.

"Drink some of this," he said.

The man raised the brandy to his lips with a hand that shook violently, and drank eagerly.

"C'est bien," he muttered, and looked from one to the other.

"I tell you this story because I am afraid to go to the police—they are watching the police office——"

"In the first place, who are you?" demanded
T. B.

"As to who and what I am," said the stranger,
nodding his head to emphasize his words, "it
would be better that I should remain silent."

"I do not see the necessity," said the detective
calmly. "So far as I can judge from what information I have, you are a French soldier—an engineer. You are a wireless telegraph operator, and
your post of duty is on the Eiffel Tower."

The man stared at the speaker, and his jaw
dropped.

"M'sieur!" he gasped.

"Hyatt was also a wireless operator; probably
in the employ of the Marconi Company in the
West of England. Between you, you surprised the
secret of a mysterious agency which employs wireless installations to communicate with its agents.
What benefits you yourself may have derived
from your discovery I cannot say. It is certain
that Hyatt, operating through Moss, made a small
fortune; it is equally certain that, detecting a
leakage, the 'Nine Men' have sent a clever agent
to discover the cause——"

But the man from the Eiffel Tower had fainted.

"I shall rely on you to keep the matter an absolute secret until we are ready," said T. B., and

the editor nodded. "I tumbled to the whole scheme when a gentleman, who shall be nameless, boasted to me that he knew certain things which it was not humanly possible for him to know—until I remembered that a certain ship was fitted with wireless telegraphy. Then it came to me in a flash. The Eiffel Tower! Who lives on the Eiffel Tower? Telegraph operators. Our friend is recovering."

He looked down at the pallid man lying limply in an armchair.

"I am anxious to know what brings him to London. Fright, I suppose. It was the death of Moss that brought Hyatt, the killing of Hyatt that produced Monsieur Escoltier."

The telegraphist recovered consciousness with a shiver and a groan. For a quarter of an hour he sat with his face hidden in his hands. Another pull at the editor's flask aroused him to tell his story —a narrative which is valuable as being the first piece of definite evidence laid against the Nine Bears.

He began hesitatingly, but as the story of his complicity was unfolded he warmed to his task. With the true Gaul's love for the dramatic, he declaimed with elaborate gesture and sonorous phrase the part he had played.

"My name is Jules Escoltier, I am a telegra-

phist in the corps of Engineers. On the establishment of the wireless telegraphy station on the
Eiffel Tower in connection with the Casa Blanca
affair, I was appointed one of the operators.
Strange as it may sound, one does not frequently
intercept messages, but I was surprised a year ago
to find myself taking code dispatches from a station which called itself 'N. H. C.' There is no such
station known, so far as I am aware, and copies
of the dispatches which I forwarded to my super-
iors were always returned to me as 'non-decod-
able.

"One day I received a message in English,
which I can read. It ran—

" 'All those who know N. H. C. call H. A.'

"Although I did not know who N. H. C. was, I
had the curiosity to look up H. A. on the telegraph
map, and found it was the Cornish Marconi Station. Taking advantage of the absence of my officer, I sent a wireless message, 'I desire information, L. L.' That is not the Paris 'indicator,' but
I knew that I should get the reply. I had hardly
sent the message when another message came. It
was from Monsieur Hyatt. I got the message distinctly—'Can you meet me in London on the 9th,
Gallini's Restaurant?' To this I replied, 'No, impossible.' After this I had a long talk with the

Cornishman, and then it was that he told me that his name was Hyatt. He told me that he was able to decode the N. H. C. messages, that he had a book, and that it was possible to make huge sums of money for the information contained in them. I thought that it was very indiscreet to speak so openly, and told him so.

"He asked me for my name, and I gave it, and thereafter I regularly received letters from him, and a correspondence began.

"Not being *au fait* in matters affecting the Bourse, I did not know of what value the information we secured from N. H. C. could be, but Hyatt said he had a friend who was interested in such matters, and that if I 'took off' all N. H. C. messages that I got, and repeated them to him, I should share in the proceeds. I was of great value to Hyatt, because I received messages that never reached him. In this way he was able to keep in touch with all the operations in which N. H. C. were engaged.

"By arrangement, we met in Paris—Hyatt, his friend of the London Bourse (Monsieur Moss), and myself, and Hyatt handed to me notes for 20,000 francs (£800); that was the first payment I received from him. He returned to England, and things continued in very much the same way as they had done, I receiving and forwarding N. H. C. messages. I never understood any of them, but Hyatt was clever, and he had discovered the code and worked it out.

"About a fortnight ago I received from him 3,000 francs in notes, a letter that spoke of a great coup contemplated by N. H. C. 'If this materializes, he wrote, 'I hope to send you half a million francs by the end of next week.'

"The next morning I received this message——"

He fumbled in his pocket and produced a strip of paper, on which was hastily scrawled—

"From N. H. C. to L.L. Meet me in London on the sixth, Charing Cross Station."

"It was, as you see, in French, and as it came I scribbled it down. I would have ignored it, but that night I got a message from Hyatt saying that N. H. C. had discovered we shared their secret and had offered to pay us £5,000 each to preserve silence, and that as they would probably alter the code I should be a fool not to accept. So I got leave of absence and bought a suit of clothing, left Paris, and arrived in London the following night. A dark young man who said his name was Silinski met me at the station, and invited me to come home with him.

"He had a motor-car at the entrance of the station, and after some hesitation I accepted. We drove through the streets filled with people, for the theatres were just emptying, and after an interminable ride we reached the open country. Silinski drove the car and I was the only other occupant. I asked him where was Hyatt, and where we were going, but he refused to speak. When I pressed him, he informed me he was taking me to a rendezvous near the sea.

"We had been driving for close on three hours, when we reached a lonely lane. By the lights of the car I could see a steep hill before us, and I could hear the roar of the waves somewhere ahead.

"Suddenly he threw a lever over, and as the car bounded forward, he sprang to the ground with a mocking laugh.

"Before I could realize what had happened, the machine was flying down the steep gradient, rocking from side to side.

"I have sufficient knowledge of motor-car engineering to manipulate a car, and I at once sprang to the wheel and felt for the brake. But both foot and hand brake were useless. In some manner he had contrived to disconnect them.

"It was pitch dark, and all that I could hope to do was to keep the car to the centre of the road.

Instinctively I knew that I was rushing to certain death, and, messieurs, I was! I was flying down a steep gradient to inevitable destruction, for at the bottom of the hill the road turned sharply, and confronting me, although I did not know this, was a stone sea wall.

"I resolved on taking my life in my hands, and putting the car at one of the steep banks which ran on either side, I turned the steering wheel and shut my eyes. I expected instant death. Instead, the car bounded up at an angle that almost threw me from my seat. I heard the crash of wood, and flying splinters struck my neck, and the next thing I remember was a series of bumps as the car jolted over a ploughed field.

"I had achieved the impossible. At the point I had chosen to leave the road was a gate leading to a field, and by an act of Providence, I had found the only way of escape.

"I found myself practically at the very edge of the sea, and in my first terror I would have given every sou I had to escape to France. All night long I waited by the broken car, and with the dawn some peasants came and told me I was only five miles distant from Dover. I embraced the man who told me this, and would have hired a conveyance to drive me to Dover, *en route* for France. I knew that N. H. C. could trace me, and then I was anxious to get in touch with Hyatt and Moss. Then it was that I saw in an English newspaper that Moss was dead.''

He stopped and moistened his lips.

"M'sieur!" he went on, with a characteristic gesture, "I decided that I would come to London and find Hyatt. I took train, but I was watched. At a little junction called Sandgate, a man sauntered past my carriage. I did not know him, he looked like an Italian. As the train left the station something smashed the window, and I heard a thud. There was no report, but I knew that I had been fired at with an air-gun, for the bullet I found embedded in the woodwork of the carriage.''

"Did nothing further happen?" asked T. B.

"Nothing till I reached Charing Cross; then when I stopped to ask a policeman to direct me to the Central Police Bureau I saw a man pass me in a motor-car, eyeing me closely. It was Silinski.''

"And then?"

"Then I saw my danger. I was afraid of the police. I saw a newspaper sheet. It was a great newspaper—I wrote a letter—and sought lodgings in a little hotel near the river. There was no answer to my letter. I waited in hiding for two days before I realized that I had given no address. I wrote again. All this time I have been seeking Hyatt. I have telegraphed to Cornwall, but the reply comes that he is not there. Then in the newspaper I learn of his death. M'sieur, I am afraid.''

He wiped the drops of sweat from his forehead with a shaky hand.

He was indeed in a pitiable condition of fright, and T. B., upon whose nerves the mysterious ''bears'' were already beginning to work, appreciated his fear without sharing it.

There came a knock at the outer door of the office, and the editor moved to answer it.

There was a whispered conversation at the door, the door closed again, and the editor returned with raised brows.

''T. B.'' he said, ''that wretched market has gone again.''

''Gone?''

''Gone to blazes! Spanish fours are so low that you'd get a pain in your back if you stooped to pick them up.''

T. B. nodded.

''I'll use your telephone,'' he said, and stooped over the desk. He called for a number and after an interval—

''Yes—that you, Mainland? Go to 375 St. John

Street, and take into custody Gregory Silinski on a charge of murder. Take with you fifty men and surround the place. Detain every caller, and every person you find in the house.''

He hung up the receiver.

"Now, my friend," he said in French, "what shall we do with you?"

The Frenchman shrugged his shoulders listlessly.

'What does it matter?" he said, "they will have me—it is only a matter of hours.''

"I take a brighter view," said T. B. cheerily; "you shall walk with us to Scotland Yard and there you shall be taken care of.''

But the Frenchman shrunk back.

"Come, there is no danger," smiled T. B.

Reluctantly the engineer accompanied the detective and the editor from the building. A yellow fog lay like a damp cloth over London, and the Thames Embankment was almost deserted.

"Do you think he followed you here?" asked T. B.

"I am sure." The Frenchman looked from left to right in an agony of apprehension. "He killed Hyatt and he killed Moss—of that I am certain— and now——"

A motor-car loomed suddenly through the fog,

coming from the direction of Northumberland Avenue, and overtook them. A man leaned out of the window as the car swept abreast. His face was masked and his actions were deliberate.

"Look out!" cried the editor, and clutched the Frenchman's arm.

The pistol that was levelled from the window of the car cracked twice and T. B. felt the wind of the bullets as they passed his head.

Then the car disappeared into the mist, leaving behind three men, one half-fainting with terror, one immensely pleased with the novel sensation— our editor, you may be sure—and one using language unbecoming to an Assistant-Commissioner of Police, for T. B. knew that the mask was Silinski, and that the detectives even now on their way to St. John Street would find the cage empty and the bird flown.

CHAPTER XVIII

THE AFFAIR OF THE "CASTILIA"

There was no apparent reason for the slump in Spanish Fours. Spanish credit never stood so high as it did at the moment of the panic. Catalonia had been appeased by the restoration of the constitution, the crops throughout Spain had been excellent, and the opening of the Porta Ciento mines, combined with the extension of the mining industry in the north, had all helped to bring about a condition of financial confidence in Spanish securities.

The "bear" attack, which was made simultaneously on every European Bourse, was, in the face of these facts, madness.

The Spanish Government rose to the situation and with praiseworthy promptness, issued broadcast warnings to the investing public. Ministers seized any opportunity for speaking on the subject of national financial stability, but the "raid" went on. No stock even remotely associated with, or dependent upon, Spain's national security was left unassailed. Telegraphs, railways, mines—they suffered in common.

Then happened that remarkable tragedy that set the whole of Europe gasping. It was a happening tragic in its futility, comic in its very tragedy. Europe was dumbfounded, speechless. There are two accounts given; there is that contained in Blue Book 7541/,09, and that issued by the Spanish Government as a White Paper. The latter, although it is little more than a reprint of a number of articles published in the *Heraldo de Madrid* and the *Correspondencia,* is as accurate and contains more detail. I have taken these accounts and summarized the story of the momentous occurrence from both.

On the morning of the 29th of January, the Spanish cruiser *Castilia* was lying in Vigo Bay. She had been engaged in gun practice on the coast, and had come into Vigo for stores and to give leave to her crew.

The ship had been coaled, ammunition and stores taken on board, and the warship steamed out to sea. Her commander was Captain Alfonso Tirez, a singularly capable officer who had served with distinction in the Spanish-American War.

The movements of the ship subsequent to her departure from Vigo Bay are fairly well known.

She was seen by a fishing fleet heading south, and was sighted level with Oporto by the Portuguese gunboat *Braganza*. More than this, she exchanged signals with the *Braganza,* making "All's well."

From this point, her voyage is something of a mystery, although it is evident that she continued a straight course.

She was not sighted again until the third of February, four days after her departure from Vigo, and the particulars of her reappearance are contained in the report made by Captain Somburn, R.N., of H.M.S. *Inveterate,* a first-class cruiser.

The *Inveterate* was detached from the Atlantic Squadron, then lying at Gibraltar, by order of the Commander-in-Chief, to cruise along the Morocco coast as far south as Mogador, and she was returning when the incident to Captain Somburn, so graphically described, occurred.

"The ship's (the *Inveterate's*) position at 7.45 was approximately Lat. 35 north and Long. 10 west, and we were due west of Cape Cantin when the *Castilia* was sighted," wrote Captain Somburn.

"She was making a course as to pass us on our starboard bow. Recognizing her, I ordered the ensign to be flown. Nothing untoward happened, and the ship came nearer and nearer.

"There had been some trouble just before I arrived at Mogador, some little fighting with a Moorish tribe, and thinking that it was on this account that the cruiser was going south, and that possibly the later news I had would be of interest to her captain, I ordered a signal to be made.

"Mogador all quiet; rising quelled."

"To my astonishment, no notice was taken of this, and not even so much as an answering pennant was hoisted.

"The officer of the watch, who had been looking at the vessel through his telescope, then reported to me that the *Castilia* was cleared for action, and that her gun crews were standing by.

"I thought that we were interrupting some manœuvre, such as 'man and arm ship,' and readily forgave her commander, who was so absorbed in his drill that he had ignored my signal.

"The next minute, however, the *Castilia* opened fire on me with her forward guns. Both shots missed, one passing our stern and the other just clearing our quarterdeck.

"I signalled 'Your firing practice is endangering me,' for, even then, I could not bring myself to a realization that the captain of the *Castilia* was in earnest.

"I was soon undeceived, however. A shell from his after four-inch gun struck and carried away a portion of the navigation bridge.

"I immediately ordered general stations, and in twenty seconds I had cleared the starboard batteries for action. In this time the *Castilia* had put three shells into the *Inveterate*. The first killed an able seaman and seriously wounded the gunnery-lieutenant, the second did little or no damage, but the third destroyed No. 3 9.6 gun and killed four of its crew.

"I at once opened fire on the *Castilia* with two six-inch guns. Both shots took effect, one, as I have since ascertained, below her water line, and she immediately heeled over to port.

"Seeing she was helpless, and sinking rapidly, I ordered away my life-boats, at the same time signalling 'I am coming to your assistance.' No further shots were fired, and the officers and crew of the *Castilia*, together with nineteen wounded men, were taken off.

"The *Castilia* sank at 8.19, the action having lasted, from the time of firing the first shot to the moment of crippling, 5 minutes, 48 seconds.

"I made no immediate attempt to ascertain the cause of the extraordinary conduct of the *Castilia*, because Captain Tirez, when I received him on board, was in a dying condition. He had been struck by a fragment of shell and never regained consciousness, expiring that afternoon, but before my arrival at Gibraltar I interviewed the Spanish officer who was acting as navigating lieutenant. From him I learned the incident was inexplicable to him, as to the rest of the crew. The captain had received a wireless telegram, coded in the secret cypher of the Admiralty. This telegram had perplexed and distressed him, but the only remark he had made to his officers had been—

" 'The Government is sending us to our deaths —but I can do nothing else than obey.'

"From this it would seem that Captain Tirez— whom I know personally to have been a very able and gallant gentleman—was acting on orders which were open to no other interpretation than as direct instructions to shell the *Inveterate*."

So much for the laconic report of the officer.

He compressed within the limits of a sheet of notepaper a tragedy, the news of which appalled the civilized world.

The battle occurred at between seven and eight

in the morning. The news was in London by ten that the *Inveterate* had been sunk by a Spanish cruiser and that a fierce and sanguinary battle had preceded its sinking.

Who sent the descriptive telegram from Gibraltar will never be known, though its source was obvious.

It bore the name of a world-famous news agency, and was issued to the Press from the London office of the Agency, but the Gibraltar correspondent had no knowledge of its sending. All England was in an uproar when the official version of the incident came to hand.

Spain! Why Spain! What was the cause? What had we done, what insult had we offered? There were writers in plenty to rush into print to prove that whatever had happened it was England's fault, but even these gentlemen could offer no elucidation.

Captain Somburn's report was telegraphed to the Admiralty immediately on his arrival at Gibraltar, and issued to the Press. Side by side in the morning newspapers appeared the official disclaimer of the Spanish Government.

"His Majesty's Government has no knowledge of any circumstance leading up to or responsible for the recent lamentable disaster off the coast of Morocco. It has issued directly or indirectly no instructions, orders, or suggestions to Captain Tirez, and has had no communication with him other than the conventional exchange of documents, peculiar to routine."

CHAPTER XIX

THE BOOK

T. B. Smith was one of many millions, who read this statement. He was one of many thousands who believed it implicitly. He was one of twelve who understood the madness of the dead Spanish Captain.

He saw, too, villainy behind it all; the greed of gold that had sent a gallant ship to the bottom, that had brought death and mutilation in most horrible form to brave men.

Silinski had slipped through his fingers—Silinski, arch-agent of the Nine.

The house in St. John Street had been raided. In a little room on the top floor there was evidence that an instrument of some considerable size had been hastily dismantled. Broken ends of wire were hanging from the wall, and one other room on the same floor was packed with storage batteries. Pursuing their investigations, the detectives ascended to the roof through a trap door. Here was the flagstaff and the arrangement for hoisting the

160

wires. Apparently, night was usually chosen for the reception and dispatch of messages. By night, the taut strands of wire would not attract attention. Only in cases of extremest urgency were they employed in daylight.

Such an occasion had been that when T. B. had interviewed Silinski. He understood now why the Pole had talked so loudly. It was to drown the peculiar sound of a wireless instrument at work.

Silinski was gone—vanished, in spite of the fact that every railway terminus in London had been watched, every ocean-going passenger scrutinized.

Now, on top of his disappearance came the *Castilia* disaster with the irresponsible public of two nations howling for a scapegoat. T. B. Smith attended a specially convened meeting of Ministers in Downing Street and related all that he knew.

"Give me two days," he said, "and you may publish the whole of the facts. But to show our hand now would be disastrous. The police of every city are engaged in tracking down the wireless stations. There is one in every capital, of that much we are sure. To get the whole gang, however, I must find out where they are operating from."

"Is that possible?" asked the grave Prime Minister.

"Absolutely, sir," said T. B.

In the end they agreed.

A more difficult man to persuade was the editor of the *London Morning Journal.*

"I have got the story, why not let me publish?" was a not unnatural request.

"In two days you shall have the complete story; what I am anxious to avoid is anything in the nature of to-be-continued-in-our-next! I want the whole thing rounded off and finished for good."

Reluctantly, the editor agreed.

He had two days to get the "book"; this code which the unfortunate Hyatt had deciphered to his undoing. Moss had said Hyatt's sister had it, but the country had been searched from end to end for Hyatt's sister. It had not been difficult to trace her. Elk, after half an hour's search in Falmouth had discovered her abode, but the girl was not there.

"She left for London yesterday," he was informed.

From that moment Miss Hyatt had disappeared.

A telegram had reached her on the very day of Hyatt's death. It said "Come."

There was no name, no address. The telegram had been handed in at St. Martin's-le-Grand; unearthed, it was found to be in typewritten characters, and the address at its back a fictitious one.

One other item of news Elk secured; there had
been a lady on the same errand as himself. "A
foreign lady," said the good folks of Falmouth.
When T. B. played the spy to the banker and the
Spanish dancer, he had heard her speak of a visit
to Cornwall; this, then, was the visit.

He had some two days to discover Eva Hyatt—
this was her name.

Silinski might have killed her; he was large in
his views and generously murderous, and one life
more or less would not count. T. B. paced his room,
his head sunk on his breast.

Where was the girl?

The telegram said "Come." It suggested some
pre-arranged plan in which the girl had ac-
quiesced; she was to leave Falmouth and go somewhere.

Who sent the telegram? Not Silinski; this Eva
Hyatt, by all showing, was of the class that sticks
for the proprieties.

Suppose she had come to London, where would
Catherine Silinski have placed her? Near at hand;
a thought struck T. B.

He had been satisfied with deporting the dancing girl, a fruitless precaution, as it turned out;
he had made no search of her flat. Had she been
arrested in the ordinary way, the search would

have followed, but her arrest was a little irregular.

He took down his overcoat and struggled into it, made a selection of keys from his pocket, and went out. It was a forlorn hope, but forlorn hopes had often been the forerunners of victory with him, and there was nothing to be lost by trying.

He came to the great hall of the mansion in Baker Street.

The hall porter recognized him and touched his cap.

"Evening, sir." Then, "I suppose you know the young lady hasn't come back yet?"

T. B. did know, but said nothing. The porter was in a talkative mood.

"She sent me a wire from Liverpool, saying that she'd been called away suddenly."

T. B. nodded. He knew this, too, for it was he who had sent the wire.

"What the other young lady couldn't understand," continued the porter, and T. B.'s heart gave a leap, "was, why——"

"Why she hadn't wired her, eh?" the detective jumped in.

"Well, you see, she was so busy——"

"Of course!" The porter clucked his lips impatiently. "Of course, you saw her off, didn't you, sir?"

"I saw her off," said T. B. gravely.

"I'd forgotten that; why, you went away together, an' I never told the young lady. She's upstairs in Miss Silinski's flat at this moment. My word, she's been horribly worried——"

"I'll go up and see her. As a matter of fact, I've come here for the purpose," said T. B. quickly.

He took the lift to the second floor, and walked along the corridor. He reached No. 43 and his hand was raised to press the little electric bell of the suite when the door opened quickly and a girl stepped out. She gave a startled cry as she saw the detective, and drew back.

"I beg your pardon," said T. B. with a smile. "I'm afraid I startled you."

She was a big florid girl with a certain awkwardness of movement.

"Well-dressed but *gauche*," mentally summarized the detective. "Provincial! she'll talk."

"I *was* a little startled," she said, with a ready smile. "I thought it was the postman."

"But surely postmen do not deliver letters in this palatial dwelling," he laughed. "I thought the hall porter——"

"Oh, but this is a registered letter," she said importantly, "from America."

All the time T. B. was thinking out some method by which he might introduce the object of his visit. An idea struck him.

"Is your mother——" she looked blank, "er—aunt within?" he asked.

He saw the slow suspicion gathering on her face.

"I'm not a burglar," he smiled, " in spite of my alarming question, but I'm in rather a quandary. I've a friend—well, not exactly a friend—but I have business with Miss Silinski, and——"

"Here's the postman," she interrupted.

A quick step sounded in the passage, and the bearer of the King's mails, with a flat parcel in his hand and his eyes searching the door numbers, stopped before them.

"Hyatt?" he asked, glancing at the address.

"Yes," said the girl; "is that my parcel?"

"Yes, miss, will you sign?"

"Hyatt?" murmured T. B., "what an extraordinary coincidence. You are not by any chance related to the unfortunate young man, the story of whose sad death has been filling the newspapers?"

She flushed and her lip trembled.

"He was my brother; did you know him?"

"I knew of him," said T. B. quietly, "but I did

not know you lived in London!"

"Nor do I," said the girl; "it is only by the great kindness of Senora Silinski that I am here."

There was no time for delicate finesse. He slid his card-case from his pocket.

"Will you let me come in and talk with you," he said; then, as he saw again the evidence of her suspicion, "I am a police-officer, and what I have to ask you is of the greatest importance to you and to me."

She took the pasteboard, and, as T. B. had anticipated, fell into a flutter of agitation.

"Oh, please come in! Was it wrong to come to London? The Senora was so anxious that nobody should know I was here. I've been so worried about her——"

She led the way into a handsomely furnished sitting-room.

"First of all," said T. B. quietly, "you must tell me how the Senora found you."

"She came to Falmouth and sought me out. It was not difficult. I have a little millinery establishment there, and my name is well known. She came one morning, eight days—no—yes, it was seven days ago, and——"

"What did she want?"

"She said she had known Charles, he had some

awfully swagger friends; that is what got him
into trouble at the post office; it was a great blow
to us because——''

''What did she want?'' asked T. B., cutting
short the loquacity.

''She said that Charles had something of hers—
a book which she had lent him, years before. Now,
the strange thing was that on the very day poor
Charles was killed I had a telegram which ran:
'If anything happens, tell Escoltier book is at Antaxia, New York.' It was unsigned, and I did not
connect it with Charles. You see, I hadn't heard
from him for years.

''She was a great friend of Charles'—the Senora—and she came down especially about the
book. She said Charles had got into trouble and
she wanted the book to save him. Then I showed
her the telegram. I was confused, but I wanted
to help Charles.'' She gulped down a sob. ''I asked
her who Escoltier was.''

''Yes?'' asked T. B. quickly.

''She said he was a friend of hers who was interested in the book. She went away, but came
back soon afterwards and told me that 'Antaxia'
was the telegraphic address of a safe deposit in
New York. She was very nice and offered to pay
for a cable to the deposit. So I wired: 'Please for-

ward by registered post the book deposited by Charles Hyatt'; and I signed it 'Eva Hyatt' and gave my address. By the evening the reply came: 'Forwarded; your previous wire did not comply with our instructions.'"

"I see," said T. B.

"Well, that is more than I can," said the girl, with a smile, "because only one wire was sent. The Senora was surprised, too, and a little annoyed, and said: 'How foolish it was of me not to ask you your Christian name.' Well, then the Senora insisted upon my coming to stay with her till the book came. I came expecting I should find Charles, but—but——"

Her eyes were filled with tears.

"I read in a newspaper that he was dead. It was the first thing I saw in London, the bill of a newspaper——"

T. B. gave her time to recover her voice.

"And the Senora?"

"She took this furnished flat near to hers," said the girl; "she lives here——"

"Does she?" asked T. B. artlessly. He took up the registered parcel which she had put on the table.

It was fairly light.

"Now, Miss Hyatt," he said, "I want you to do

something for me; and I must tell you that, although I ask it as a favour, I can enforce my wishes as a right.''

''I will do anything,'' said the girl eagerly.

''Very well; you must let me take this book away.''

''But it is not mine; it belongs to the Senora,'' she protested; ''and it is to save my brother's name——''

''Miss Hyatt,'' said T. B. gently, ''I must take this book which has so providentially come into my hands, not to save your brother's name, but to bring to justice the men who took his life.''

As he spoke there came a knock at the door; and, hastily drying her eyes, the girl opened it.

A porter handed her a telegram, and she came back into the light of the room to open it.

She read it, and re-read it; then looked at T. B. with bewilderment written on her face.

''What does this mean?'' she said.

T. B. took the telegram from her hand; it had been re-addressed from Falmouth, and ran:

''By wireless from Port Sybil. Do not part with book to anybody on any account,
                    ''CATHERINE SILINSKI.''

T. B. handed the telegram back.

"It means," he said, "that our friend is just two minutes too late."

CHAPTER XX

AT THE ADMIRALTY

Wherever men met they spoke of one thing; they had one subject of conversation; in train or in club-room; in bar or meeting-place, in barristers' robing-room; in prisoners' waiting hall—the *Castilia,* and Spain.

Small doubt but that there were demands, irresponsible demands for satisfaction, after satisfaction had been given. But tangible satisfaction was needed. Spain had dared . . . insult to the might and majesty of Britain—war must be a logical outcome—and the like.

These outpourings appeared in many newspapers under the heading, "Letters to the Editor." Some newspapers would not print them because of a curious resemblance between them.

The Editor of the *London Journal* made this discovery.

The *Journal* is a newspaper controlled by a great syndicate which owns a newspaper in every one of the great centres of industry throughout

Great Britain. It has a system of exchanging confidences, and, as a result, it was found that a letter addressed to *The Northern Journal and Times* was identical, word for word, with a letter addressed to the London paper. With this difference, that whilst one was signed "J. Y. Barver," the other bore the magnificent signature of "Orlando T. Sabout." The editor sent both letters to T. B. Smith, and T. B. grinned unpleasantly, but with some admiration for the completeness of the Nine Men's organization.

On top of these letters, was revived a form of publicity which had long since fallen into desuetude—the pamphlet was mooked.

Three pamphlets were shot suddenly into the market. This was the second day after the sinking of the *Castilia*.

One, the more virulent, was called "A Blow at Protestantism," and was an invitation to England to sweep Europe clear of the "Catholic menace."

Neither pamphlet could have been written in two days. They must have been prepared a fortnight to a month in advance of the disaster. They bore no publisher's imprint or printer's advertisement.

"This business is a little too hot to hold," said

the editor in a final interview with T. B. "To-night I must tell the whole of the story."

T. B. nodded.

"To-night," said T. B., "you can tell what you like. I shall have played my stake for good or ill."

"I have been talking with Escoltier; we have got him lodged in Scotland Yard—though you needn't mention that fact in your account—and I think we know enough now to trap the Nine Men."

"Who are they and what does the 'C' stand for in 'N. H. C.'?"

"I can only guess," said T. B. cautiously. "Do you know anything about wireless telegraphy?" he demanded.

"Not much," admitted the editor.

"Well, you know enough to realize that the further you wish to communicate the more electrical energy you require?"

"That much I understand," said the journalist. "The principle is the 'rings on the pond.' You throw a stone into still water, and immediately rings grow outward. The bigger the stone, the farther reaching the rings."

"At Poldhu," continued T. B., "Hyatt was in charge of the long-distance instrument. As a matter of fact, the work he was engaged on was merely experimental, but his endeavour seemed to be centred in securing the necessary energy for communicating nine hundred miles. Of course, wireless telegraphy is practicable up to and beyond 3,000 miles, but few installations are capable of transmitting that distance.

"So 'C' is, you think, within 900 miles of Cornwall?"

T. B. nodded.

"I have a feeling that I know 'C'," he said. "I have another feeling that these wireless messages do not come from 'C' at all, but from a place adjacent. However,"—he took from his pocket a flat exercise book filled with closely-written columns of words and figures—"we shall see."

He took a cab from Fleet Street; and, arriving at the block of Government buildings which sheltered the Lords Commissioners of the Admiralty, he entered its gloomy doors.

A messenger came forward to inquire his business, but was forestalled by a keen little man with tanned face and twinkling eyes. "Sailor" was written on every line of his mahogany face. "Hullo, my noble policeman!" he greeted T. B. "Who is the victim—the First Sea Lord or the Controller of the Victualling Department?"

"To be precise, Almack," said T. B. "I have

come to arrest Reform, which I gather——''

"No politics," smiled Captain John Almack, R.N. "What is the game?"

"It is what our mutual friend Napoleon would call a negative problem in strategy," the Assistant-Commissioner replied. "I want to ask an ethereal friend, who exists somewhere in space, to come in and be killed."

Captain Almack led the way up a flight of stairs.

"We got a request from your Commissioner; and, of course, the Lords of Admiralty are only too pleased to put the instrument at your disposal."

"They are very charming," murmured T. B.

"They instructed me to keep a watchful eye on you. We have missed things since your last visit.

"That sounds like a jovial lie," said T. B. frankly.

In the orderly instrument room they found an operator in attendance, and T. B. lost no time.

"Call N. H. C.," he said; and, whilst the instrument clicked and snapped obedient to the man's hand, T. B. opened his little exercise book and composed a message. He had finished his work long before any answer came to the call. For half an hour they waited whilst the instrument clicked monotonously. "Dash-dot, dot-dot-dot, dash-dot-dash-dot."

And over and over again.

"Dash-dot, dot-dot-dot, dash-dot-dash-dot."

Then suddenly the operator stopped, and there came a new sound.

They waited in tense silence.

"Answered," said the operator.

"Take this." T. B. handed him a slip of paper.

As the man sent the message out with emphatic tappings, Captain Almack took the translation that T. B. handed him.

"To N. H. C. There is trouble here. I must see you. Important. Can you meet me in Paris to-morrow?"

After this message had gone through there was a wait of five minutes. Then the answer came, and the man at the instrument wrote down unintelligible words which T. B. translated.

"Impossible. Come to M. Will meet S. E. Have you got the book?"

"Reply 'Podaba'," instructed T. B., spelling the word. "Now send this." He handed another slip of paper across the table, and passed the translation back to the man behind him.

"Is Gibraltar intercepting messages?" it ran Again the wait, and again the staccato reply.

"Unlikely, but will send round tomorrow to make sure. Good-night."

As the instrument clicked its farewell, T. B. executed a silent war-dance to the scandal of the solemn operator, and the delight of the little captain.

"T. B., you'll get me hung!" he warned. "You'll upset all kinds of delicate instruments, to say nothing of the telegraphist's sense of decency. Come away."

"Now," demanded Captain Almack, when he had led him to his snug little office; "what is the mystery?"

T. B. related as much of the story as was necessary, and the officer whistled.

"The devils!" he swore. "And so that's the explanation of the poor old *Castilia's* sinking is it?"

"The discovery I was trying to make," T. B. went on, "was the exact location of N. H. C. I asked him or them to come to Paris. As a matter of fact, I wanted to know if they were within twenty-four hours' distance of Paris. 'Impossible,' they reply. But they will come to Madrid, and offer to meet the Sud Express. So they must be in Spain and south of Madrid, otherwise there would be no impossibility about meeting me in Paris tomorrow. Where are they? within reach of

Gibraltar apparently, because they talk of sending round tomorrow. Now, that phrase 'sending round' is significant, for it proves beyond the shadow of a doubt exactly in what part of Andalusia they live.''

"How?"

"When people who live within reach of the fortress talk of going to Gibraltar, as you know, they either say that they are 'going across to Gibraltar' or that they are 'going round.' By the first, they indicate the route *via* Algeciras and across the bay; by the latter, they refer to the journey by way of Cadiz and Tangier——"

"Cadiz!"

The exclamation came from his hearers.

"Cadiz," repeated T. B. He bent his head forward and rested it for a moment in his hands. When he lifted it, they saw that his face was grave.

"It's worth trying," he muttered. "And," he continued aloud, "it will be bringing down two birds with one stone."

"May I use the instrument again?" he asked.

"Certainly," said the officer readily.

T. B. rose.

"I'm going to Scotland Yard, and I shall not be away for more than ten minutes," he said; and in a few seconds he was crossing Whitehall at a run.

He passed through the entrance and made straight for the big bureau, where day in and day out the silent recorder sat with his pen, his cabinets and his everlasting *dossier*.

T. B. knew he would be there, because there was a heavy calendar at the Old Bailey, and the silent man was working far into the night—arranging, sorting, and re-arranging.

The detective was back at the Admiralty within the ten minutes, and together the two made their way to the Instrument Room.

"N. H. C." responded almost at once, and T. B. sent his message.

"Tell George T. Baggin that another warrant has been issued for his arrest."

The reply came immediately.

"Thanks. Get further particulars, but do not use names."

T. B. read the reply and handed it without a word to the other.

"Please God, I'll hang the man who sent that message," he said, with unusual earnestness.

CHAPTER XXI

SILINSKI STRIKES

It was half-past nine when T. B. sent and received the last message; and an hour later he had interviewed the Commissioner.

"Get your lady away all right?" his chief greeted him.

"Well away, sir," said T. B. serenely. "Out of reach of Silinski—his agents were watching the flat—there was a burglary there the very night the book arrived."

"And the lady?"

"She is due in Jamaica in a few days."

"And now——"

T. B. told the story of the developments.

The Commissioner nodded from time to time.

"You're an ingenious young man," he said. "One of these fine days somebody will badly want your blood."

"It has often happened," T. B. granted. "There was Spedding, the forger; you remember him, sir?

There was—oh, I could give you a dozen instances.''

He sat over a companionable cigar and a whisky and soda, talking until the hands of the clock were near on midnight; then he rose to take his leave.

"You will leave for Spain tomorrow?" asked the Chief.

"Yes; by the first train. I can get the warrants from the Yard before I leave, and the Spanish authorities will give me all the help I need."

"And what of Silinski?" asked the Chief Commissioner.

T. B. shrugged his shoulders.

"We had a murderer there," he said. "I am satisfied that with all his *alibis*, he killed Moss. Whether he actually stabbed Hyatt, I am not sure. The man had such a perfect organization in London that it is possible that one of his cut-throat friends served him in the case of that unfortunate young man. Silinski can wait. If we get the others, we shall get him."

"Good-night, sir."

He grasped the proffered hand, and his host ushered him into the silent street.

He took two steps forward, when a man rose apparently from the ground, and two shots rang out. T. B. had drawn his revolver and fired from his hip, and his assailant staggered back cursing as a dark shadow came running from the opposite side of the road to his help.

Then T. B. swayed, his knees bent under him, and he fell back into the Commissioner's arms.

"I'm done," he said, and the third man, whose name was Silinski, hesitating a moment in the roadway, slipped his revolver back into his pocket and fled.

CHAPTER XXII

THE CONVICT FROM CEUTRA

The streets of Cadiz were deserted; only by the Quay was there any sign of life, for here the crew of the Brazilian warship, the *Maria Braganza*, were languidly embarking stores on flat-bottomed lighters, and discussing, with a wealth of language and in no complimentary terms, the energy of their commander. It was obvious, so they said in their picturesque language, that a warship was never intended to carry cargo, and if the Brazilian Government was foolish enough to purchase war stores in Spain, it should go a little farther, and charter a Spanish merchant ship to carry them.

So they cursed Captain Lombrosa for a dog and the son of a dog, and predicted for him an eternity of particular discomfort.

Captain Lombrosa, a short, swarthy man, knew nothing of his unpopularity, and probably cared less. He was sitting in the cafe of the Five Nations, near the Plaza de Mayor, picking his teeth thoughtfully and reading from time to time the

184

cablegram from his Government which informed
him that certain defalcations of his had been discovered by the Paymaster-General of the Navy,
and demanding peremptorily his return to Rio de
Janeiro.

To say that Captain Lombrosa was unperturbed
would be to exaggerate. No man who builds his
house upon sand can calmly regard the shifting
foundations of his edifice. But he was not especially depressed for many reasons. The Government
had merely anticipated events by a week or so.

He read the cablegram with its pencilled deco-
dation, smiled sadly, put up his feet on a chair,
and called for another bottle of Rioja.

There is an unlovely road through the dreary
waste that leads from Cadiz to San Fernando.
Beyond the city and beyond the Arsenal the road
winds through the bleak salt marshes to Jerez,
that Xeres de la Fonterra which has given its
name to the amber wine of Spain.

A solitary horseman cantered into San Fernando, his clothing white with brackish dust. He
drew rein before the Cafe Cruz Blanca and dis-
mounted; an untidy barefooted boy leading his
horse away.

There were few people in the saloon of the
cafe, for a chill wind was abroad, and the *cappa*

is a very poor protection against the icy breezes that blow from the Sierras.

A man greeted the horseman as he entered—an outrageously stout man with bulging cheeks and puffy eyes. He breathed wheezily, and his fat hands moved with a strange restlessness.

They hailed each other in the Andalusian dialect, and the new comer ordered "*Cafe c'leche.*"

"Well, friend?" asked the stout man, when the waiter had disappeared. "What is the news?"

He spoke in English.

"The best," replied the other, in the same language. "T. B. is finished."

"No!"

"It's a fact."

"Ramundo shot him at close range, but the devil went down fighting. They've got Ramundo."

The fat man snorted.

"Isn't that dangerous?" he asked.

"For us, no; for him, yes," said the man carelessly. "Ramundo knows nothing except that he has been living in the lap of luxury for two years in London on the wages of an unknown employer."

"What will he get?" asked the stout man nervously.

The man looked at him curiously.

"You are getting jumpy, friend Meyers," he said coolly.

"I am getting sick of this life," said Meyers. "We're making money by the million, but what is the use of it? We are dogs that dare not show our noses abroad; we're exiled and damned and there is no future."

"You might as well be here as in prison," philosophized his friend. "And in prison you most certainly would be, if not worse——"

"We had no hand in the murders," interrupted Meyers pleadingly. "Now did we, Baggin?"

"I know little about the English law," drawled George T. Baggin, sometime treasurer of the London and Manhattan Securities Syndicate. "But such knowledge as I have enables me to say with certainty that we should be hanged—sure."

The fat man collapsed, mopping his brow.

"Ramundo killed one and Silinski the other," he mumbled. "What about Silinski?"

"He was standing by when T. B. was shot; but, as soon as he saw the policeman was down and out, he skipped. He arrives tonight."

Some thought came to him which was not quite agreeable, for he frowned.

"Silinski, of course, knows," he went on meditatively. "Silinski is one with us."

"He has been a good servant," the fat man ventured.

"Had been," said the other, emphasizing the first word.

"What do you mean? Was it not he who established our stations and got the right men to work 'em? Why, he has got the whole thing at his fingers' ends."

"Yes," agreed Baggin, with a wry smile. "And he has us at his fingers' ends also—where are our friends?—the other matter I have arranged without calling in Silinski."

"They are returning tonight." The fat man shifted uncomfortably. "You were saying about this T. B. fellow—he is dead?"

"Not dead, but nearly; Silinski saw him carried into the house, and a little later an ambulance came flying to the door. He saw him carried out."

Meyers lowered his voice.

"Is Silinski——?" He did not complete his sentence.

"He's dangerous. I tell you, Meyers, we are on tender ice; there's a cracking and a creaking in the air."

Meyers licked his dry lips.

"I've been havin' dreams lately," he rumbled. "Horrid dreams about prisons——"

"Haw—cut it out," said the disgusted American. "There's no time for fool dreaming. I'm going to the committee tonight; you back me up. Hullo?"

A beggar had sidled into the Cafe in the waiter's absence. He moved with the furtive shuffle of the practised mendicant.

His hair was close cropped, and on his cheeks was a three days' growth of beard.

He held out a grimy hand.

"Senor," he murmured. "Por Dios——"

"Git."

The man looked at him appealingly.

"Diez centimos, Senor," he whined.

Baggin raised his hand, but checked its descent. He had seen something behind the ragged jacket closely buttoned at the throat.

"Wait for me on the road to Jerez," he commanded, and tossed the man a silver piece. The beggar caught it with the skill of an expert.

The American cut short the torrent of thanks, blessings, and protestations.

"Meet me in half an hour; you understand?"

'What the devil are you going to do?" demanded Meyers.

"You shall see."

Half an hour later they emerged from the Cafe,

Baggin to his horse, and the fat man to a capacious victoria, that he had summoned from the hotel stables.

A mile along the road they came up with the beggar.

"Get down, Meyers, and send the victoria on; you can signal it when you want it."

He waited until the empty victoria had driven away; then he turned to the waiting ragamuffin.

"What is your name?"

"Carlos Cabindez," said the man hesitatingly.

"Where do you live?"

"At Ronda."

"Where have you come from?"

"Tarifa."

"What is your trade?"

The man grinned and shuffled his feet.

"A fisherman," he said at last.

Baggin's hand suddenly shot out; and, grasping his collar, tore open the frayed jacket.

The man wrenched himself free with an imprecation.

"Take your hand from that knife," commanded Baggin. "I will do you no harm. Where did you get that shirt?"

The beggar scowled and drew the threadbare coat across his chest.

"I bought it," he said.

"That's a lie," said Baggin. "It's a prisoner's shirt; you are an escaped convict."

The man made no answer.

"From Ceutra?"

Again no reply.

"What was your sentence? Answer."

"Life," said the other sullenly.

"Your crime?"

"*Asesinatos.*"

"How many?"

"*Tres.*"

Baggin's eyes narrowed.

"Three murders, eh?" he said. "Then you would like to earn a thousand pesetas?" he asked.

The man's eyes lit up.

"You can go on, Meyers," he said. "I shall see you tonight. In the meantime, I wish to have a little talk with our friend here."

CHAPTER XXIII

THE HOUSE ON THE HILL

Beyond the town of Jerez and on the road that runs westward to San Lucar, there is a hill. Once upon a time, a grey old watchtower stood upon its steepest place, but one day there came an eccentric American who purchased the land on which it stood, demolished the tower, and erected a castellated mansion. Rumour had it that he was mad, but no American would be confined on a Spaniard's appreciation of sanity.

The American consul at Jerez, of his charity and kindliness of heart, journeyed out to call upon him, and received a cold welcome. A message came to him, but the proprietor was in bed with gout, and neither then or at any time desired visitors, which so enraged the well-meaning consul that he never called again. The American's visits were of a fleeting character. He was in residence less than a month in the year. Then one day he came and remained. His name was registered as Senor Walter G. Brown, of New York. The Eng-

lish police sought him as George T. Baggin, an
absconding promoter, broker, bucket-shopkeeper,
and all-round thief. After a time he began to receive visitors, who stayed on also.

Then came a period when Mr. Walter G. Brown
became aggressively patriotic.

He caused to be erected on the topmost tower
of his mansion an enormous flagstaff, from which
flew on rare occasions a ridiculously small Stars
and Stripes.

At night, the place of the flag was taken by a
number of thick copper strands, and simple-
minded villagers in the country about reported
strange noises, for all the world like the rattling
of dried peas in a tin canister.

On the evening of a wintry day, many people
journeyed up the steep pathway that led to the
mansion on the hill. They came singly and in pairs,
mostly riding, although one exceedingly stout man
drove up in a little victoria drawn by two panting
mules.

The last to come was Mr. Baggin, an unpleasant
smile on his square face.

By the side of his horse trotted a breathless
man in a tattered coat, his cropped head bare.

"I will show you where to stand," Baggin said.
"There is a curtain that covers a door. The man

will pass by that curtain, and I shall be with him. I will hold his arm—so. Then I will say 'Senor Silinski I do not trust you,' and then——"

The ragged man swept the sweat from his forehead with the back of his hand, for the path was steep.

"And then," he grunted, "I will strike."

"Surely," warned the other.

The man grinned.

"I shall not fail," he said significantly.

They disappeared into the great house—it is worthy of note that Baggin opened the door with a key of his own—and darkness fell upon the hill and upon the valley.

Far away, lights twinkling through the trees showed where Jerez lay.

CHAPTER XXIV

THE NINE BEARS

The room in which the Nine Men sat was large even as rooms go in Spain. It had the appearance of a small lecture hall. Heavy curtains of dark blue velvet hid the tall windows, and electric lights, set at intervals in the ceiling, provided light.

The little desks at which the men sat were placed so as to form a horseshoe.

Of the nine, it is possible that one knew the other, and that some guessed the identity of all. It was difficult to disguise Meyers with his unwieldy bulk, yet with all the trickery of the black cloaks they wore and the crepe masks that hid their faces, it was hard enough to single even him from his fellows.

The last man had reached his seat when one who sat at the extreme end of the horseshoe on the president's right, rose and asked: "What of Silinski, brother?"

"He has not yet arrived," was the muffled reply.

"Perhaps, then, it is well that I should say what I have to say before his return," said the first speaker.

He rose to his feet, and eight pairs of eyes turned towards him.

"Gentlemen," he began, "the time has come when our operations must cease."

A murmur interrupted him, and he stopped.

"What is it?" he asked sharply.

"Let us have more light," said a mask at the end of the horseshoe, and pointed to the ceiling where only half of the lights glowed.

Baggins nodded, and the man rose and made his way to the curtained recess where the switches were.

"No, no, no!" said Baggin quickly—for he suddenly realized that there was something hidden by the curtain, a sinister figure of a man in convict shirt, fingering the edge of a brand new knife. So Baggin pictured him.

The masked man halted in surprise.

"No, no," repeated Baggin, and beckoned him back. "For what I have to say I need no light; you interrupt me, brother."

With a muttered apology the man resumed his seat.

"I have said," continued Baggin, "that the time has come when we must seriously consider the advisability of dispersing."

A murmur of assent met these words.

"This organization of ours has grown and grown until it has become unwieldy," he went on. "We are all business men, so there is no need for me to enlarge upon the danger that attends the house that undertakes responsibilities which it cannot personally attend to.

"We have completed a most wonderful organization. We have employed all the ingenuities of modern science to further our plans. We have agents in every part of Europe, in India, Egypt, and America. So long as these agents have been ignorant of the identity and location of their employers, we were safe. To ensure this, we have worked through M. Gregory Silinski, a gentleman who came to us four years ago—under peculiar conditions.

"We have employed, too, and gratefully employed, Catherine Silinski, a charming lady, as to whose future you need have no fear. Some time ago, as you all know, we established wireless stations in the great capitals, as being the safest method by which our instructions might be transmitted without revealing to our agents the origin of these commands. A code was drawn up, certain arrangements of letters and words, and this code was deciphered and our secret revealed through the ingenuity of one man. We were prepared to meet him on a business basis. We communicated with him by wireless, and agreed to pay a sum not only to himself, but to two others, if he kept our secret and agreed to make no written record of their discovery. They promised, but their promise was broken, and it was necessary to employ other methods.

"I am fully prepared to accept responsibility for my share of the result, just as I am prepared to share responsibility for any other act, which circumstances may have rendered necessary.

"And now, gentlemen, I come to the important part in my speech. By sharing the result of our operations we may each go our way, in whatever guise we think most suitable, to the enjoyment of our labours.

"In a short time for many of us the Statute of Limitations will have worked effectively; and for others there are States in South America that would welcome us and offer us every luxury that money can buy or heart desire.

"Yet I would not advise the scattering of our forces. Rather, I have a scheme which will, I think, enable us to extract the maximum of enjoyment from life, at a minimum of risk. With that end in view, I have expended from our common fund a sum equal to half a million English pounds. I have completed elaborate arrangements, which I shall ask you to approve of; I have fashioned our future." He threw out his hands with a gesture of pride. "It is for you to decide whether we shall go our several ways, each in fear of the weakness of the other, our days filled with dread, our nights sleepless with doubt, or whether in new circumstances we shall live together in freedom, in happiness, and in unity.

Again the murmured applause.

"But there is an element of danger which must be removed," Baggin went on, "between freedom and us there lies a shadow."

He stopped and looked from mask to mask.

"That shadow," he said slowly, "is Gregory Silinski, the man who knows our secret, who has done our work, the one man in the world who holds our lives in the hollow of his hand."

Before he had finished he saw their eyes leave his face and seek the door, and he turned to meet the calm scrutiny of the subject of his discourse.

He entered the room whilst Baggin was speaking and stood listening.

Silinski had an air of his own; a deferential, yet menacing air, which impressed you. He had been described by T. B. Smith as a combination of head-waiter and hangman—not an unhappy description.

Now he stood with eyes fixed on Baggin.

"Monsieur Baggin does me an honour that I do not deserve," he said suavely, in his high lisping voice.

Baggin shot a swift side glance at a curtained recess behind which stooped a crop-haired man in a convict shirt, fingering a brand-new knife.

"Monsieur Baggin," Silinski went on, "is wrong when he says I am the only man who stands between the Nine Bears of Cadiz and freedom—there is another, and his name is T. B. Smith."

"T. B. Smith is dead, or dying," said Baggin angrily, "we have your word for it."

Silinski favoured him with the slightest bow.

"Even Silinski may fall into an error," he said magnanimously. "T. B. is neither dead nor hurt."

"But he fell?"

Silinski smiled.

"It was clever, and even I was deceived," he confessed; "the ambulance that took him away was an artistic conception—he is alive and——"

He walked forward until he was opposite the curtain where the assassin waited.

"He is in Jerez, messieurs."

"It's a lie," shouted Baggin. "Strike, Carlos."

He wrenched the curtain aside, revealing the sinister figure behind.

Silinski fell back with an ashen face, but the convict made no move.

Baggin sprang at him in a fury, and struck madly, blindly, but Silinski's arm caught his, and wrenched him backward.

In Silinski's other hand was a revolver, and the muzzle covered the convict.

"Gentlemen," said Silinski, and his eyes blazed with triumph, "I have told you that T. B. Smith was alive—behold him!"

And T. B. Smith, in his convict shirt, standing with one hand against the wall of the recess, and the other on his hip, smiled cheerfully.

"That is very true," he said.

Under his hand were the three switches that controlled the light in the room.

"It is also true," said Silinski, who dearly loved a speech, "that you are virtually dead."

T. B. nodded; he knew his man by now.

"Wasn't it a Polish philosopher," he began

with all the hesitation of one who is beginning a long discourse, "who said——"

Then he switched out the light and dropped flat on the floor. The revolvers cracked together, and Silinski uttered an oath.

There was a wild scramble in the dark. A knot of men swayed over a prostrate form; then a trembling hand found the switch, and the room was flooded with light.

Silinski lay flat on his back with a bullet through his leg, but the man they sought, the man in the striped shirt and with a three days' growth of beard, was gone.

CHAPTER XXV

T. B. SMITH REPORTS

In red, blue, and green; in type varying in size according to the temperament of the newspapers; in words wild or sedate, as the character of the journal demanded, the newspaper contents bills gave London its first intimation of the breaking up of the Nine Bears.

"Never in the history of our time," began the leading article of the *Telegram*.

"A story which reads like the imaginative conception of the romantic writer," began the leader of the *London Times and Courier*.

That the Nine Bears were dispersed was hailed as a triumph for the English police. Unfortunately, the popular view is not always the correct view, and T. B. Smith came back to London a very angry man.

It had been no fault of his that the majority of the band had escaped.

"The Civil Guard was twenty minutes late in taking up its position," wrote T. B. in his private report.

"No blame attached to the Guard, which is one of the finest police forces in the world, but of the local police authorities, who at the eleventh hour detected some obscurity in their instructions from Madrid, and must needs telegraph for elucidation. So that the ring about the House on the Hill was not completed until long after the whole lot had escaped. We caught Francois Zillier, who has been handed over to the French police, but the remainder of the gang got clean away. Apparently they have taken Silinski with them; he may or may not be dangerously wounded, but such indications as we have point to his having been badly hurt. How the remainder managed to carry him off passes my comprehension; the 'why' of it is apparent. He knows too much. We have secured a few documents. There is one mysterious scrap of paper discovered in Baggin's private room which is incoherent to a point of wildness, and apparently the rough note of some future scheme; it will bear re-examination."

CHAPTER XXVI

THE LADY WHO LOST £200

There was, in the Record Office at Scotland Yard, and is probably still, a stout package containing a number of telegrams written in French, English, Spanish, German, Portuguese and Italian. Each one of these wires is to the same effect as the others.

"Exhaustive enquiries throughout the country have failed to discover any trace of the Nine Bears of Cadiz."

The story of these men, inscribed in the records of Scotland Yard, is not perhaps as complete as that in the possession of the French police, for M. Escoltier, some time confidential wireless operator of the Eiffel Tower, had placed the police of Paris in possession of a great deal of useful information that he had denied the Metropolitan authorities.

From the rough notes of the telegrams he had received and transmitted to the unfortunate Hyatt, the French police, with the aid of codes obligingly supplied by Scotland Yard, had been able to grasp the magnitude of the operations conducted by the Nine. The extent of these operations revealed the extraordinary thoroughness of their organization. In various names, and under cover very often of innocent-looking commercial concerns, they had conducted their nefarious business with impunity. There is now no doubt whatever that the Deutsch Ost-Amerika Handel, with its gorgeous offices at The Hague, was part of the chain of operating centres. Equally certain it is that the Compagnie de Maritime de Solent was another. The Credit Sud-Espagna — despite threats of libel actions—was a third. One could multiply the list, covering bogus concerns in Vienna, Petersburg, Moscow, Milan, Rome, Budapest, Bukarest, and Brussels.

So far as we have been able to trace, there was no office in Copenhagen or in either of the Scandinavian capitals. By means of M. Escoltier's telegrams the French police made an approximate estimate of the extent of the profits secured by the band:

Slump in Kaffirs (anticipating the announcements that the Portuguese Government refused recruiting facilities for native labour)....£1,750,000

Slump in New York steel (anticipating the "suicide" of the President of the National Bank of Baltimore) £2,850,000
Slump in copper..£1,340,000
(Coincident with the arrest of Mr. Hilas B. Cuttering on a charge of misappropriation. The documents on which the arrest was effected were afterwards discovered to be forgeries) £1,000,000
Slump in British Industrials (expert opinions hold that this was one of the failures of the Nine) £100,000
Slump in Spanish Fours............................£2,000,000
(See page 49 of the Appendix of M. Gaultier's Report.)

It well may be that the French police have overestimated the hauls, just as they have entirely failed to connect the disastrous fall of Argentine securities with the revolution of '07—a revolution which owed its origin to the machinations of the Nine Men of Cadiz.

The discovery of the band and the revelations of its *modus operandi* must stand as the greatest sensation in the history of crime. It was followed by the world-famous "International Convention of 1910," and the adoption of its recommendation prohibiting the working of private wireless instruments without a licence from the Government,

making any breach of the ordinance a penal offence.

"Thanks to the industry and perseverance of
the English police," said the *London Morning
Journal,* commenting upon this law, "the Nine
Men of Cadiz are dispersed, their power destroyed, their brilliant villainies a memory. It is
only a matter of time before they will fall into
the hands of the police, and the full measure of
Society's punishment be awarded them. Scattered
as they are——"

T. B. Smith put down his paper when he came
to this part, and smiled grimly.

"Scattered, are they!" he said. "I doubt it."

For all the praise that was lavished upon him
and upon his department, he was not satisfied with
himself. He knew that he had failed. To break up
the gang had always been possible. To arrest them
and seize the huge fortune they had amassed
would have been an achievement justifying the
encomia that was being lavished upon him.

"The only satisfaction I have," he said to the
Chief Commissioner, "is that we are so often
cursed for inefficiency when we do the right thing,
that we can afford to take a little credit when
we've made a hash of things."

"I wouldn't say that," demurred the Chief.

"You did all that was humanly possible."

T. B. sniffed.

"Eight men and Silinski slipped through my fingers," he answered briefly; "that's a bad best."

He rose from the chair and paced the room, his head sunk on his breast.

"If Silinski had delayed his entrance another ten minutes," he said, stopping suddenly. "Baggin would have told me all that I wanted to know. This wonderful scheme of his that was to secure them all ease and security for the rest of their lives."

"He may have been boasting," suggested the other, but T. B. shook his head.

"It was no boast," he said, with assurance, "and if it were, he has made it good, for where are the Nine? One of them is on the Devil's Island, because he had the misfortune to fall into our hands. But where are the others? Vanished! Dissolved into the elements—and their money with them. I tell you, sir, there is not even the suspicion of a trace of these men. How did they get away from Cadiz? Not by rail, for all northward trains were stopped at Bobadilla and searched. Not by sea, for the only ship that left that night was the Brazilian man-o'-war, *Maria Braganza.*"

"Airship," suggested his Chief flippantly, as he moved towards the door.

"It is unlikely, sir," replied T. B. coldly.

The Chief Commissioner stood with his hand on the edge of the open door.

"At any rate, they are finished," he said, "their power for further mischief is destroyed."

"I appreciate your optimism, sir," said T. B. impertinently, "which I regret to say I do not share."

Three months had passed since the disappearance of the "bears"; from that day no news had come which might even remotely associate them with a hiding-place.

"One thing is evident, and must be remembered," T. B. went on, as his Chief still lingered. "Outside of the Nine Men there must be in Europe hundreds of agents, who without being aware of their principals, have been acting blindly for years in their interest. What of the men who went to the length of murder at Silinski's orders? What of the assassins in Europe and America who 'arranged' the suicide of the Bank President and the wreck of the Sud Express? Not one of these men have we been able to track down. I tell you, sir, that outside of the inner council of this gang, Silinski organized as great a band of villains as the world has ever seen. They remain; this is an indisputable fact; somewhere in the world, scat-

tered materially, but bound together by bonds of
Silinski's weaving, are a number of men who
formed the working parts of the Nine Men's great
machine. For the moment the steam is absent—
Yes?''

A constable was at the door.

"There is a lady to see you, sir," he said.

"Lady?" said T. B. wonderingly, for ladies
were rare amongst his regular callers. "What does
she want?"

"I don't know, sir, except that she wants to see
you about some money," said the man.

T. B. looked up at his Chief in blank astonishment, and the elder man shook his head sadly.

"I should never have suspected you, T. B.," he
said sorrowfully, with which cryptic utterance he
left T. B. alone to his interview.

The lady was stout and voluble, respectable,
middle class. Her ample bosom was a chaos of
brooches, ranging in size from a half-crown to a
coffee saucer. She was red of face and scant of
breath, and with a gracious inclination of her
head she took the seat to which T. B. motioned her.

"Mr. Smith?"

T. B. nodded, and the lady fumbled in a little
black satin bag that hung from her wrist. It contained many things that rattled; it also contained

a little notebook, which the lady extracted and opened.

"On the 4th ultimo," she began.

"May I ask, madam," interrupted T. B. Smith, with some little evidence of irritation, "exactly what your business is?"

The lady shot at him a look in which reproof and indignation were blended.

"I have some experience of the police," she said bitingly, "having given evidence against Gustav Heilberg, a house-boy charged at the West London Sessions with having stolen a ring valued at four guineas, the property of——"

"But——"

"The legal mind," she said, with a magnanimous sweep of her hand, "is not beyond my comprehension, 'These police officials are busy people; they want all the facts set forth clearly, concisely'—er, another word begins with 's' which has for the moment escaped me—yes, 'succinctly,' that is it."

"To all this I agree," said T. B.; he walked to his desk and pressed a bell. "If it is another case of Gustav Heilberg, I will see that you are escorted to the proper department. I do not deal with these matters myself——"

"Stop!" The lady raised a gleaming hand .

"This is a matter of greater importance—it concerns you—and a lady."

If his visitor intended shocking him she succeeded admirably.

T. B.'s eyebrows rose, his lean jaw dropped.

"A matter of two hundred and fifty-five," said madam, holding her head till the ornament of her bonnet shivered again, "advanced to a friend of yours last week—I say advanced, because I want no unpleasantness. I think that it is right to explain that we were fellow-passengers—the money never left me day or night, being always wrapped up in my nightdress bag, placed under the pillow——"

"I see!" A light was beginning to dawn on T. B. "You have been robbed and somebody has told you to come to me——"

"Wait," said the lady imposingly; "wait; by day I carried it in my bodice—such a nice gal she was, used to sit for hours talking about my late husband, and her brother was such a gentlemanly man with a little peaky beard and eyeglasses, like a young man I used to know at the Hydro at Malvern. Well, she talked and talked, she helped me with my packing; I went down to help her with hers, though she never asked me, and," said the lady, wagging an impressive finger; "the first thing I saw in her cabin was you."

"Eh?"

T. B. stared at the lady blankly.

"You," repeated the visitor, with evidence of the satisfaction that her startling news produced. "You as large as life; in a silver frame, propped up on the bunk."

" 'Who's that?' says I.

" 'A friend of mine,' says she, snatching up the photo. That was all. But I have a memory for faces; the other day I saw your portrait in the *Police News*——"

T. B. made a little grimace.

"I saw your portrait in the *Police News*," she repeated, "and I says to myself, 'Ah, ha, my lady! I'm going to call on this friend of yours.' "

She paused and looked triumphantly at the detective.

"Two hundred and fifty-five pounds in Bank of England notes," she said slowly, emphasizing each word with a jab of her right finger in the palm of her left hand. "Gone!"

"When did you find this out?"

T. B. was interested now, although filling in the spaces of her disjointed narrative, he perceived

little more than a fairly common story of an
ordinary theft.

"When I got to Euston the money was in my
jewel-case; my card-case was packed in it, and I
wanted to give my card to a very charming girl
I met in the train—niece of a Lord Somebody or
other—I opened the case—gone!"

Again she stopped.

"Well?" said the detective. "What do you expect me to do?"

"Find my money," said the lady complacently.
"If she knows you, you must know her."

"What was her name?"

"Mad'moozle de Verdum."

The detective shook his head.

"I don't know the name," he said, "and if I
did, I don't suppose I could find her; you may be
sure that if she is a professional thief she has left
England——"

"She is here; I saw her today. I was on the top
of a 'bus, and she was in a carriage," said the
lady bitterly, "paid for out of my money; you
don't know her name, de Verdum?"

"I do not," said T. B., and rose to signify that
the interview was finished.

"Suppose she had another name; suppose the
name I saw on a card in her cabin was her name?"

"In that case," said T. B. wearily, "you had better give me that also."

For a moment the lady groped in the recesses of her satin bag, and after what looked like developing into an interminable search, she produced a card.

"Here it is," she said, and read:

" 'Catherine Silinski.' "

CHAPTER XXVII

IN THE RECORD OFFICE

T. B. spun round as though the lash of a whip had caught him.

"Silinski — Catherine Silinski — here?" he breathed.

"Here!" said the triumphant lady. "Now, will you tell me that you can't get my money back?"

"It's incredible, unthinkable!"

Silinski in London!

As he stood, his mind busily engaged in speculation, his visitor grew impatient.

"Two hundred and fifty-five pounds," she murmured absently.

He looked up.

"Your money, madam," he said briskly, "is the least important aspect of the question."

The lady was not unnaturally annoyed.

* * * *

The little telegraph instrument near the chief inspector's desk began to click. In every police station throughout the Metropolis it snapped forth

217

its message. In Highgate, in Camberwell, in sleepy
Greenwich, in Ladywell, as in Stoke Newington.
"Clickerty, clickerty, click," it went, hastily,
breathlessly. It ran:

"To all Stations:—Arrest and detain man and
woman (here the descriptions followed) on a
charge of having stolen bank-notes to the amount
of £255 from Louisa Breddell, of Sloe Grove,
Bayswater. All reserves out in plain clothes."

All reserves out!

That was a remarkable order. What was the importance of this theft of £255 that the whole of
the London police force should be mobilized to find
the thief?

London did not know of the happening; the
homeward-bound suburbanite may have noticed a
couple of keen-faced men standing idly near the
entrance of the railway station, may have seen a
loiterer on the platform—a loiterer who apparently had no train to catch. Curious men, too, came to
the hotels, lounging away the whole evening in the
entrance hall, mildly interested in people who
came or went. Even the tram termini were not
neglected, nor the theatre queues, nor the board-
ing-houses of Bloomsbury. Throughout London,
from East to West, North to South, the work that
Scotland Yard had set emissaries to perform, was

swiftly and expeditiously carried out.

T. B. sat all that evening in his office waiting. One by one little pink slips were carried in to him and laid upon the desk before him.

As the evening advanced they increased in number and length.

At eight o'clock came a wire:

"Not leaving by Hook of Holland route."

Soon after nine:

"Continental mail clear."

Then in rapid succession the great caravanserai reported themselves. Theatres, bars, restaurants, every place in London where men and women gather together, sent, through the plain-clothes watchers, their messages.

T. B.'s hope lay in the woman. Without her, Silinski might hide himself in some obscure slum in the Metropolis. At eleven o'clock he was reading a telegram from Harwich when the telephone, at his elbow buzzed.

He took up the receiver.

"Hullo," he said curtly.

For a second there was no reply, and then, very clear and distinct, came a voice.

"T. B. Smith, I presume."

It was the voice of Silinski.

If there had been anybody in the room, but T. B.

they might have imagined it was a very ordinary call he was receiving. Save for the fact that his face twitched, as was a characteristic of his when labouring under any great excitement, he gave no sign of the varied emotions Silinski's voice had aroused.

"Yes, I am T. B. Smith; you are, of course, Silinski?"

"I am, of course, Silinski," said the voice suavely, "and it is on the tip of your tongue to ask me where I am."

"I am hardly as foolish as that,' said T. B. drily; "but wherever you are—and I gather from the clearness of your voice that you are in London—I shall have you."

There was a little laugh at the other end of the wire.

T. B.'s hand stole out and pressed a little bell-push that rested on the table.

"Yes," said Silinski's voice mockingly. "I am in London. I am desirous of knowing where my friends have hidden."

"Your friends?" T. B. was genuinely astonished.

"My friends," said the voice gravely, "who so ungenerously left me to die on the salt plains near **Jerez** whilst they were making their escape."

A constable entered the room whilst Silinski was talking, and T. B. raised his hand warningly.

"Tell me," he said carelessly, "why you have not joined them."

Then, like a flash, he brought his hand down over the transmitter and turned to the waiting constable.

"Run across to Mr. Elk's room," he said rapidly; "call the Treasury Exchange and ask what part of London—what office—this man is speaking to me from."

Silinski was talking before T. B. had finished giving his instructions.

"Why have I not joined them," said Silinski, and there was a little bitterness in his voice, "because they do not wish to have me. Silinski has served his purpose. Where are they now? that is what I wish to know. More important still, I greatly desire a piece of information which you alone, senor, can afford me."

The sublime audacity of the man brought a grin to T. B.'s face.

"And that is?" he asked.

"There was," said Silinski, "amongst the documents you found at our headquarters in Jerez a scrap of paper written somewhat unintelligibly, and apparently—I should imagine, for I have not seen it—without much meaning.''

"There was," said T. B. cheerfully.

"So much I gathered from Baggin's agitation on our retreat," said Silinski. "Where, may I ask, is this interesting piece of literature deposited?"

The cool, matter-of-fact demand almost took T. B.'s breath away.

"It is at present at Scotland Yard," he said.

"With my—er—*dossier?*" asked the voice, and a little laugh followed.

"Rather with the *dossier* of your friend, Baggin," said T. B.

"In case I should ever want to burgle Scotland Yard," said the drawling voice again, "could you give me explicit instructions where to find it?"

T. B.'s anxiety was to keep Silinski engaged in conversation until the officer he had dispatched to the telephone returned.

"Yes," he said, "at present it is in the cabinet marked 'Unclassified Data,' but I cannot promise you that it will remain there. You see, Silinski, I have too high an opinion of your enterprise and daring."

He waited for a reply, but no reply came, and at that moment the door opened and the constable he had sent on the errand appeared.

T. B. covered the transmitter again.

"The Treasury say that you are not connected with anybody, sir," he said.

"What?"

T. B. stared at him.

He moved his hand from the transmitter and called softly, "Silinski."

There was no reply, and he called again.

He looked up with the receiver still at his ear.

"He's rung off."

Then a new voice spoke.

"Finished, sir?"

"No, who are you?" demanded T. B. quickly.

"Exchange, sir—Private Exchange, Scotland Yard."

"Who was talking to me then? Where was he talking from?"

"Why, from the Record Office."

T. B., his face white, leaped to his feet.

"Follow me," he said, and went racing down the long corridor. He went down the broad stairs three at a time.

A constable on duty in the hall turned in astonishment.

"Has anybody left here recently?" asked T. B. breathlessly.

"A gentleman just gone out, sir," said the man;

"went away in a motor-car—lady driving."

"Is Mr. Elk in the building?"

"In the Record Office, sir," said the man.

Up the stairs again flew the detective. The Record Office was at the far end of the building.

The door was ajar and the room in darkness, but T. B. was in the room and had switched on the light.

In the centre of the room was stretched the unfortunate Elk, in a pool of blood. A life-preserver lay near him. T. B. leant over him; he was alive, but terribly injured; then he shot a swift glance round the room. He saw the telephone with the receiver off; he saw an open cabinet marked "Unclassified Data," and it was empty.

CHAPTER XXVIII

THE LOST WARSHIP

Translation of an Extract from a little memorandum book found in Gregory Silinski's house in St. John Street and now in possession of the Police Authorities.

"It may be said that life is fairly crude, from the standpoint of the professional writer, and 'True Stories' have a singular knack of being remarkably dull.

"Thus in actuality it very often happens that *dénouements* have a knack of postponing themselves for a dozen years or so—a dozen years that enables the hero to grow fat and the heroine to lose a little of the bloom of youth and develop characteristics which are not in harmony with one's original conception of her character.

"Very few indeed of the stories, tragic or comic, of real life, make good 'book tales,' because life is made up of anti-climaxes, and because the villains of life more often than not live to be respected, and virtue so frequently goes to the wall

before an unappreciative world can realize its im
mense and gratifying worth.''

One need not be an admirer of Silinski to agree
with the truth of much that he has said.

Silinski was a philosopher, without being a
gentleman.

It may be that on the slender basis of his philo-
sophy he depended too implicitly. He would argue
that since his case was one of actuality he was
safe in putting back the *dénouement* for a dozen
years or so. More he may have entertained visions
of a respectable old age—of a Silinski white-
haired, benevolent, and venerated, musing in his
dotage of virtuous competitors buried and forgotten.

Unfortunately, the story of the ''Nine Bears'' is
a ''book'' story—one of a very few, and the *dénouement* came with disconcerting swiftness. To
such comfort as he might extract from his philo-
sophy he was welcome.

T. B. Smith was a philosopher, but of another
type; his attitude in the face of blame was one of
stoical equanimity; before a too lavish award of
praise he was cynically tolerant.

There might have been blame in plenty, if the
news of the outrage at Scotland Yard leaked out,

but, fortunately, Elk was not killed and the world was unaware of the happening.

Silinski had escaped; there was pother enough; eight of the Nine Bears had melted into nothingness; no official feather came to T. B.'s cap for that, whatever praise the mistaken public might award. Worst of all, the Record Office at Scotland Yard had been burgled and important documents had been stolen.

Their contents were not lost to the police, for Scotland Yard does not put all its eggs into one basket, even when the basket is as secure a one as the Record Office. There were photographs innumerable of the scrap of paper, and one of these was on T. B. Smith's desk the morning after the robbery.

The memorandum, for such it was, was contained in less than a hundred words. Literally, and with all its erasures written out, it ran:

"Idea (crossed out). Ideas (written again). Suppose we separated; where to meet; allowing for accidental partings; must be some spot; yet that would be dangerous; otherwise, must be figures easily remembered; especially as none of these people have knowledge (crossed out and re-written); especially as difficult for non-technical (word undecipherable) to fix in mind, and one cipher makes all difference. LOLO be good, accessible, unfrequented. Suggest on first Ju every year we rendezvous at Lolo.

("Mem.—Lolo would indeed be nowhere!)

"So far have only explained to Zillier."

That was all, and T. B. read and re-read the memorandum. Zillier was the only man who knew. By the oddest of chances, Baggin had confided his plans to the one man who might have found them useful if Providence had given him one chance of escape. But the French Government had him safe enough on Devil's Island.

For the rest, the "note" needed much more explanation than he could give it.

He took a pen and began to group the sentences he could not understand.

"Must be some spot, yet that would be dangerous; otherwise must be figures easily remembered."

A spot would be dangerous? He was perplexed, and showed it. What was meant by "spot"?

He grinned faintly, remembering a famous legal quibble as to what was a "place" within the meaning of an Act. Any given point on the earth's surface was a "spot," so what could the "otherwise" mean? Somewhere that was not on the earth? He

smiled again. In the air? What were the figures—
and technical figures at that?

"On the 1st of Ju we rendezvous at Lolo—nowhere!"

"This is absolute nonsense!" The detective
threw down his pen and jumped up. "I'll go over
to the hospital and see old man Elk."

He called at the Chief Commissioner's office and
was received cordially.

"Any news, T. B.? what do you make of your
puzzle?"

T. B. made a little grimace.

"Nothing," he said, "and if the original had
not been stolen I should not have troubled to study
it."

He gained the Strand by a short cut.

A contents bill attracted his attention, and he
stopped to buy an evening newspaper.

"LOSS OF A WARSHIP"

He turned the paper before he discovered the
small paragraph that justified so large a bill.

"The Brazilian Government has sent another
cruiser to search for the Brazilian man-of-war,
Maria Braganza, which is a month overdue. It is
feared that the warship foundered in the recent
cyclone in the South Atlantic."

"Maria Braganza?" thought T. B.—and remembered where he had seen the vessel.

The ship and her fate passed out of his mind soon afterward, for he had a great deal of routine work requiring his attention; but the name cropped up again in the course of the day and in a curious manner.

*   *   *   *

A drunken sailor, obviously of foreign extraction, was ejected, fighting from a small public-house in the Edgware Road. He rose from the ground slowly, and stood apparently debating in his mind whether he should go away quietly or whether he should return to the attack. It is not too much to say that had he decided upon the pacific course, the mystery of the whereabouts of the Nine Bears might never have been elucidated. In that two seconds of deliberation hung the fates of Baggin and his confederates, of Silinski and his sister, indeed of the reputation of Scotland Yard.

The foreign sailor made up his mind. Back to the swing doors of the tavern he staggered, pushed them open and entered.

A few minutes later a police whistle blew, a commonplace constable strolled leisurely to the scene of the disturbance and took into custody the pugnacious foreigner on a charge of "drunk and disorderly."

This was the beginning of the final fight with the "bears," a fight which cost Europe a million of money and many lives, but which closed for ever the account of the Nine Bears of Cadiz.

CHAPTER XXIX

SILINSKI UNDERSTANDS

What "double chambers" are to the dramatist, parallel columns are to the journalist; in the former you see two actions going on at the same time, in the latter you may observe two minds working differently to the same end.

Thus Gregory Silinski of Paris and T. B. Smith in London.

You may picture Silinski on a day in April, when Paris was awakening to spring-time, and the branches of the trees in the Bois de Boulogne vivid green. A day very balmy, with a hint of early summer, with no bite in the breeze that came in soft gusts along the Boulevard des Capucines.

Every day to the *Coq d'Or* came a thoughtful student, clean-shaven, dressed in shabby black, with a cravat sufficiently extravagant to suggest art, and spectacles business-like enough to hint at medicine. This Monsieur Flamarrion lived in the

Montmartre, and described himself as a mechanical engineer. He was—so said his papers—from Bayonne.

He came, naturally enough, under the observation of the police, and was reported to be a bachelor of "studious and virtuous" habits; he had, said the report, *"ne pas ami intime."* Your Parisian detective, by nature suspicious, differs materially from his brother at Scotland Yard. In the first place, he concentrates his attentions too fiercely and is too readily swayed by first impressions. Under his terrific scrutiny and examinations the newly observed takes on a permanent character. Thus M. Flamarrion, a newcomer to Paris, endured the embarrassing attention of the French police for exactly two days, and was passed as "harmless."

And all this time, T. B. Smith was imploring the French authorities to keep a strict watch on Silinski. Every day came M. Flamarrion to soak his *brioch* in his coffee and read patiently and thoroughly the *Journal des Débats.*

Every day, too, to this admirable tavern came a young lady, heavily veiled and wearing the evidence of recent widowhood.

They did not sit at the same table, but generally

they were near enough to exchange furtive glances and conventional politeness.

"May I offer you *Le Matin*, madame?"

"I am obliged to you, monsieur."

Thus would Silinski communicate with his sister, for always, with the newspaper he so politely tendered, would be a letter giving her his news, his plans, and such money as she required.

This April morning Catherine read her note with some trepidation. There was a little flush on Silinski's cheek when he greeted her, his eyes were a thought too bright, and his nod lacked the pretence of deference which usually marked it.

More than this, he threw away all pretence of strangership and called her to his table.

"Catherine," he said quickly, "we must leave Paris."

She nodded.

"Our friend, Zillier!" he said, dropping his voice. "Consider it, little one! Whilst we are at liberty he languishes on in chains! A prisoner, a dog!"

She looked at him curiously.

His eyes were dancing, that little patch of red was in his face; she knew they stood on the threshold of a great enterprise.

"I cannot sleep at nights," he went on. "I start up and see Zillier in his cage——"

"Gregory," she said steadily, "why do you talk thus to me?"

He was not abashed.

"Little one," he said exultantly, "I talk thus because I feel thus. Zillier means a return to the grip of things. Baggin has gone, and with him my good fortune; you cannot any more secure employment; we have had to descend to petty robberies to sustain life. The Nine Men I made!" he said, and, since the café was empty, he indulged in his favourite gesture. "I created them, their machinery, their organization, their very code. And now——! I have on my hands a hundred and one bold gentlemen who, their fortunes being bound in mine, find their means of living gone. On the one hand, I am sought by the police, who want my life, on the other by my agents, who want my money—of the two I fear the police least."

He paused to sip his coffee.

"From police and friends I have one refuge—the Nine Men of Cadiz; now the eight men of nowhere and the one of Devil's Island. How to join forces—how to reach Mr. Baggin, that is the question."

He took a scrap of paper from his pocket-book.

"This was valueless to me until to-day," he said, tapping the paper. "It gave me no clue as to the means by which my friends escaped, vanished into the void; but to-day has come a great light. We go to join our friends!"

So much for Silinski, who, as we now know, left Paris that night.

CHAPTER XXX

WHAT THE SAILOR SAID

The solution of the "note" did not come so quickly to T. B., because his mind could not jump as Silinski's did.

"Here is a case that will amuse you, T. B.," said the Chief, strolling into his bureau; "a man, giving the name of Silva, who has been taken to the police-station on the prosaic charge of 'D. and D.', is found to be a walking cash deposit. Twelve hundred pounds in Bank of England notes and 26,000 francs in French money was found in his possession. He speaks little or no English, has the appearance of being a sailor—will you go down and see what you can make of him?"

In a quarter of an hour the Assistant-Commissioner was at the police-station.

"Yes, sir," said the station sergeant, "he's quiet now. I don't think he's so very drunk, only pugilistically so."

"What do you make of him?"

"He's a sailor; a deserter from some foreign navy, I should say. He has underclothes of a uniform type, and there's a sort of device on his singlet—three stars and a number."

"Brazilian Navy," said T. B. with promptness. "Talkative?"

The sergeant smiled.

"In his own language, very," he said drily. "When I searched him, he said a great number of things which were probably very rude."

T. B. nodded.

"I'll see him," he said.

A gaoler led him down a long corridor.

On either side were long stone-painted doors, each with a little steel wicket.

Stopping before one door, he inserted his bright key in the lock, snapped back a polished bolt, and the door swung open.

A man who was sitting on a wooden bench with his head in his hands, jumped to his feet as the Assistant-Commissioner entered, and poured forth a volume of language.

"Softly, softly," said T. B. "You speak Spanish, my friend."

"Si, senor," said the man. "I am Spanish."

"That is good, for I cannot speak Portuguese," said T. B.

"I know nothing of Portuguese," said the man quickly.

"Yet you are a deserter from a Brazilian warship," said T. B.

The man stared at him defiantly.

"Is not that so, friend?"

The prisoned shrugged his shoulders.

"I should like to smoke," was all that he said.

T. B. took his gold case from an inside pocket and opened it.

"Many thanks," said the sailor, and took the lighted match the gaoler had struck.

If he had known the ways of the English police, he would have grown suspicious. Elsewhere, a man might be bullied, browbeaten, frightened into a confession. In France, Juge d'Instruction and detective would combine to wring from his reluctant lips a damaging admission. In America, the Third Degree, most despicable of police methods, would have been similarly employed.

But the English police do most things by kindness, and do them very well.

The sailor puffed at his cigarette, from time to time looking up from the bench on which he sat at the detective's smiling face.

T. B. asked no questions; he had none to ask; he did not demand how the man came by his wealth; he would not be guilty of such a crudity. He waited for the sailor to talk. As last he spoke.

"Senor," he said, "you wish to know where I got my money?"

T. B. said nothing.

"Honestly," said the sailor, loudly, and with emphatic gesture, "honestly, senor," and he went on earnestly, "By my way of reckoning a man has a price."

"Undoubtedly," agreed T. B.

"A price for body and soul." The sailor blew a ring of smoke and watched it rise to the vaulted roof of the cell.

"Some men," continued the man, "in their calm moments set their value at twenty million dollars —only to sell themselves in the heat of a foolish moment for——" he snapped his fingers.

"I have never," thought T. B., "come into contact with so many philosophical criminals in my life."

"Yet I would beg you to believe," said the sailor—and I would ask the reader to realize that he was speaking in Spanish, which gives even to the uneducated speech a certain literary pedantry —"it is a question of opportunity and need. There are moments when I would not risk my liberty for a million pesetas—there have been days when I would have sold my soul for ten mil-reis."

He paused again, for he had all the Latin's appreciation of an audience; all the Latin's desire for dramatic effect.

"Sixty thousand pesetas is a large sum, senor; it amounts to more than £2,000 in your money—that was my price!"

"For what?"

"I will set you a riddle: on the *Maria Braganza* we had one hundred officers and men——"

T. B. saw light.

"You are a deserter from the *Maria Braganza*," he said—but the man shook his head smilingly.

"On the contrary I have my discharge from the navy, properly attested and signed by my good Captain. You will find it at my lodgings, in a tin trunk under a picture of the blessed Saint Teressa of Avila, or, as some say, Sergovia. No, senor officer, I am discharged honourably. Listen."

His cigarette was nearly finished and T. B. opened his case again, and the man, with a grateful inclination of his head, helped himself. Slowly he began his story, a story which before all others, I think, helps the mind to grasp the magnitude of a combination which made the events he described possible.

"I was a sub-officer on the *Maria Braganza*," he

began, and went on to narrate the history of the voyage of that remarkable battleship from the day it left Rio, until it steamed into the roadstead off Cadiz.

"We stayed at Cadiz much longer than we expected, and the men were grumbling—because our next port was to have been Rio. But for some reason our Captain did not wish to sail. Then one day he came on board—he spent most of his time ashore—looking extremely happy. Previous to this he had lived and walked in gloom, as though some matter were preying on his mind. But this was all changed now. Whatever troubles he had were evaporated. He walked about the deck, smiling and cracking jokes, and we naturally concluded that he had received his orders to sail back to Brazil at once.

"That same day we were ordered to take on board stores which the government had purchased. Whatever stores these were, they were extremely heavy. They were packed in little square boxes, strongly made and clamped with steel. Of these boxes we took two hundred and fifty, and the business of transporting them occupied the greater part of a whole day."

"What was the weight of them?" asked T. B.

"About fifty kilos," said the man, "and," he

added, with an assumption of carelessness, "they each contained gold."

T. B. did a little sum in his head.

"In fact a million and a half of English pounds," he said half to himself.

"As to that I do not know," said the other, "but it was enormous; I discovered the gold by accident, for I and another officer had been chosen to store the boxes in one of the ammunition flats, and owing to the breaking of a box I saw—what I saw."

"However, to get back to the Captain. In the evening he came aboard, having first given orders for steam to be ready and every preparation made for slipping."

"Then it was I told him I had seen the contents of one of the boxes, and he was distressed.

" 'Who else has seen this?' he asked, and I informed him of the sub-officer who had been with me.

" 'Do not speak of this matter, as you value your soul,' he said, 'for this is a high Government secret—send sub-officer Alverez to me'—that was the name of my companion. I obeyed and sent Alverez aft. He too, received similar injunctions, and was dismissed.

"At ten o'clock that night, the quarter-masters went to their stations, and all stood ready for dropping our mooring.

"As the hours wore on, the Captain began to show signs of impatience. I was on the bridge with the officer of the watch, and the Captain was pacing up and down, now looking at his watch and swearing, now training his binocular on a portion of the land to the north of the town.

"I had forogtten to say that at 8.30 the ship's steam pinnace had been sent away, and that it had not returned.

"It was for the coming of the pinnace, and whoever was coming with it, that our Captain displayed so much anxiety.

"It was eleven o'clock before the boat came alongside. We heard it racing across the water— for the night was very still. Then it drew alongside, and a number of gentlemen came on board. They were all talking excitedly, and seemed as though they had walked a long distance, for, by the light of the branch lamp that lit the gangway I saw that their boots and trousers were white with dust, such as I believe lies on the road outside Cadiz. One was in a state of great fear; he was very stout. Another, and he was the leader, spoke to our Captain, and soon after I heard the order given—'Quartermaster, stand by for going out of harbour,' and the Captain gave the navigating officer his course. We went out at full speed, steering a course due west.

"It was a perfectly calm night, with stars, but no moon. When (as near as I can guess) we were twenty miles from the coast, the Captain sent for me and Alverez to his cabin.

" 'My friends,' he said, 'I have a proposition to make to you, but first let me ask you if you are good patriots?'

We said that we were.

" 'What,' said the Captain, addressing himself to me, 'do you value your patriotism at?'

I was silent.

"Senor," said the prisoner earnestly, "I assure you I was not considering the insult offered to me, because we had got to a point outside of abstract morality. In my mind was a dilemma— if I ask too little I should assuredly lose money. Such was also the consideration in Alverez's mind. 'Senor Captain,' I said, 'as an honest man——'

" 'We will leave that out of the question,' said the Captain. 'Name a price.'

"And so, at random, I suggested a sum equal

to £3,000, and Alverez, not a man of any originality, repeated '£3,000.'

"The Captain nodded; 'This sum I will pay you,' he said. 'Moreover, I will give you your discharge from the navy of Brazil, and you may leave the ship tonight.'

"I did not ask him why. I realized he had some high scheme which it was not proper I should know, besides which I had not been ashore for a month—and there was the £3,000.

" 'Before you go,' said the Captain, 'I will explain to you that my honour and my reputation may not suffer. In a few days' time, when we are at sea, the comrades you leave behind will be offered a new service, a service under a new and wealthier Government, a Government that will offer large and generous rewards for faithful service and obedience.' "

The prisoner chuckled softly, as at some thought which amused him.

"We went ashore in the steam pinnace; the Captain himself superintending our landing. It was a remarkable journey, senor.

"You may imagine us in the open sea, with nothing but the 'chica-clucka, clucka!' of the engine of our little boat; Alverez and myself sitting

at the bow with our hands on the butts of our revolvers—we knew our Captain—and he himself
steering us for the lights that soon came up over
the horizon. We landed at Cadiz, and were provided with papers to the Brazilian Consul, should
our return be noticed. But none saw us, or if they
did, thought nothing of the spectacle of two Brazilian seamen walking through the streets at that
hour of the night; remember that none but the
port authorities were aware that the *Maria Braganza* had sailed. The next morning we procured
some civilian clothing, and left by the afternoon
train for Seville. By easy stages we came first
to Madrid, then to Paris. Here we stayed some
time."

He chuckled again.

"Alverez," he resumed, "is a man of spirit,
but, as I have said, of no great originality. In
Paris a man of spirit may go far, a man of money
farther, always providing that behind the spirit
and the wealth there is intelligence. My poor Alverez went his own way in Paris. He made
friends."

Again he smiled thoughtfully.

"Alverez I left," he explained; "his ways are
not my ways. I came to England. I do not like
this country," he said frankly. "Your lower

classes are gross people, and very quarrelsome.''

A few more questions were asked, and answered, and ten minutes later T. B. was flying back to Scotland Yard with the story of the stolen battleship.

CHAPTER XXXI

THE "MARIA BRAGANZA"

Once more were the Nine Men in the bill of every newspaper in London. Once more the cables hummed from world's end to world's end, and slowly, item by item, came fragmentary scraps of news which Scotland Yard pieced together.

"Of all extraordinary developments," said the *London Journal*, "in any great criminal case, nothing has ever equalled in its improbability, the present phase of this remarkable case. Our readers will remember . . . "(here the *Journal* went on to give the story of the inception and progress of the Nine Men in their schemes—a story with which the reader is already familiar).

"And now we have reached the stage which we confidently hope will be a final one. It is clear that these men, having command of enormous riches, gained at the sacrifice of life, and by the ruin of thousands of innocent people, secured to their service the Captain of the Brazilian warship, *Maria Braganza.*

"Captain Lombroza holds an unenviable reputation in the Brazilian navy. A Court of Inquiry had discovered that, for years, he had been systematically robbing the Brazilian Treasury, and the discovery of his speculation coincided with his disappearance; but not only with his disappearance but with the vanishing of the Brazilian Government's battleship.

"It is not difficult to understand what arguments the Nine Men used to win over the crew of this unfortunate battleship. They had enormous wealth at their command; they could offer to pay salaries which, to the untutored men of the Brazilian Navy, must have seemed beyond the dreams of avarice.

"But what is the explanation of the discharge of Alverez and his companion?

"To our minds it would seem tolerably easy. These two men of all the crew knew the extent of the riches brought on board the *Maria Braganza.* They of all the crew had a comprehension of the wealth of the Nine Men. They were dangerous men to have on board; their presence might mean mutiny, strikes, all the extraordinary consequences of a position which would be Gilbertian were it not for the note of tragedy that underlies the whole remarkable story.

"From the day the *Maria Braganza* left Cadiz it has, apparently, been lost to sight. We say 'apparently' because a closer inspection of shipping records leads us to the belief that this ship has not only been sighted, but has coaled at a British port. On the 16th of January, Lloyds published, amongst other arrivals, that of the *Spinoza* at Port Elizabeth. At first, this was reported to be a warship flying the flag of Venezuela. This was later corrected to Colombia, a mistake very easy to make if one were to judge the nationality of a ship by its ensign; for, save for a small emblem in the centre of the flags, both these countries display a similar ensign. A reference to the battle-ships of the world, shows us that no such warship exists, and later advices from the Cape go to prove that the vessel that came in, coaled and took stores so hurriedly, was none other than the *Maria Braganza*. So that somewhere in the wide seas of the world is a stolen battleship, having on board a congregation of the world's worst rascals, Napoleonic in the largeness of their crimes. But money, which can do much, cannot do all, and it is necessary that these men, no less than the ship's company, should obtain stores and food, and the necessities of life; more important still, that they should secure the coal that is so necessary a part of the ships equipment. In this respect we have made one or two important discoveries.

"An examination of the shipping list shows that two months ago three colliers were chartered out of Cardiff. There is nothing remarkable in this fact, and their apparent destination excited no comment at the time. They were ordered to very usual ports in South America, but it is an extraordinary fact that the consignor in each case gave the captain sealed orders which were only to be opened at sea. So far, we have had no news from these ships, and it is the merest conjecture on our parts when we suppose the colliers were intended for the *Maria Braganza* and, that at some rendezvous, and at some appointed time, they were met by the warship in mid-ocean, and there transferred their cargo.

"But more mysterious is the chartering of the *Hedleigh Head,* a tramp steamer of 2,000 tons, which took on board, on the 16th of last month, one of the strangest cargoes that ship has ever taken. We now know that a month prior to this, one of the largest furnishing firms of the West End received an order to the extent of £10,000, for the delivery of elaborate ship's fittings, intended,

as it was said, for a South American yacht owner.
The firm in question makes a specialty of such
luxurious appointments, and such an order was
not regarded as unusual, and so chairs, panels, up-
holstery of all kinds, paints, mouldings, and twelve
magnificent cabin suites were placed on board the
Hedleigh Head, and were ostentatiously consigned
to Valparaiso. Here, again, the captain received
sealed orders, and here again we think we are justified in assuming these goods were intended for
the *Maria Braganza;* and that, so far from the
ship's destination being Valparaiso, the cargo was
met on the high seas and taken over.

"Many and fantastic are the suggestions that
have been put forward as to the whereabouts of
the Nine Men of Cadiz. One of our contemporaries
draws a fanciful picture of life on some gorgeous
Southern Pacific Isle, out of the track of steamers,
and pictures the Nine Men living in a condition of
Oriental splendour, an existence of *dolce far
niente.* Such a supposition is, of course, on the
face of it, absurd. Such an island exists only in the
fancy of the romantic writer. The uninhabited por-
tions of the globe are few, and are in the main, of
the character of the Sahara desert. Wherever life
can be sustained, wherever comfort and freedom
from disease waits the newcomer, be sure the new-

comer has already arrived."

I quote this much from the *Journal* because it is near enough to truth and actuality to merit quotation.

That Baggin had based all his plans on the supposition that such an island existed, and could be discovered, we now know. He was the possessor of an imagination, but his geographical knowledge was faulty.

The "idea," that scrap of paper which Silinski had risked his neck to obtain, was simple enough now—up to a point.

THE "IDEA"

"Suppose we separated, where to meet? Must be some spot yet that would be dangerous."

THE SOLUTION

"Some spot," meant some place on land.

"Otherwise, must be easily remembered. Especially as it is difficult for non-technical (?) to fix in mind, and one cypher makes all the difference."

The latitude and longitude of sea rendezvous must be easy to remember.

"Suggest we rendezvous at Lolo."

This last was the only part of the little clue that offered any difficulty to T. B. The *Gazetteer* supplied no explanation.

Nor could the Admiralty help. The naval authorities did their best to unravel the mystery of "Lolo."

T. B., who saw no reason to suppress such news as he had, and following the precedent he had established when he revealed the story of the deserter to the Press, called that engine to his aid, and all newspaperdom racked its brains to discover in "Lolo," a cryptic reference to some lonely Pacific island.

Many and ingenious were the suggestions offered, but none found favour.

A conference of the Ambassadors met in London, and it was jointly agreed that the nations should act in concert to bring the *Maria Braganza* and her crew to justice as speedily as possible. The Brazilian Government agreed to indemnify the Powers in their action, and in the event of the destruction of the ship being necessitated by resistance on the part of its rebel captain, to accept an agreed sum as compensation.

There are surprising periods of inaction in the record of all great accomplishments, which those who read the stories of achievements, realize.

There were weeks of fretting, and days of blank despair in one room at Scotland Yard. For the examination of all clues led to the one end. Somewhere in the world were the Nine Men of Cadiz— but where none could say. Every port in every civilized land was alert. Captains of mail steamers, of grimy little tramps, of war vessels of every nation, watched for the battleship. Three British cruisers, detached unostentatiously from the Home Fleet, cruised unlikely seas, but with no good result.

Then began the new terror.

T. B. had always had one uncomfortable feeling, a feeling that the dissipation of the Nine had not dispelled, and that was the knowledge that somewhere in Europe the machinery set up with devilish ingenuity by Silinski, still existed. Who were the desperate and broken men who acted as agents to the Nine? Whoever they were, they had been well chosen.

Silinski possessed an extraordinary acquaintance with the criminal world. There was scarcely a land in which he had not been a sojourner, a citizen of the shades, more often than not, a fugitive of justice.

That he then had a splendid opportunity of meeting with the very type which was ultimately to prove of such value to him, there can be no doubt.

Investigations had not brought any of these men to the light of day; they lurked in the background —ominous, menacing, a constant danger.

That danger was all the greater if Silinski had rejoined his accomplices, or if by any chance he had come into touch with them, as he boasted he had.

This knowledge of danger was irritating, more irritating since it ran with the impatience engendered by inaction. For three weeks—three whole eternities—no word came of the *Maria Braganza;* then a Cape steamer picked up a ship's boat with a dead man and a rough wooden chest filled with English gold-coins. There were no papers, no name was painted on the little boat, but for the mystery of the tragic find T. B. had a solution which received official support. One of the crew of the *Maria Barganza* had looted the treasure and attempted to steal away by night. He had succeeded only too well.

"This suggests," said T. B., "that at the time of the desertion the warship was within sailing distance from some coast, probably the isle of Sao Thome or Principe. The man, having no com-

pass, took a wrong course; from the description
he must have died of thirst.''

Two gunboats from the Cape station were sent
to search those latitudes, but drew blank. The commander of the *Dwarf*, a small British gunboat,
however, was partially successful, for it fell in
with a Monrovian fishing-boat which had sighted
a ''big steamer'' three weeks before, heading
south.

The British Government had taken every precaution to prevent supplies reaching the Nine. It
was forbidden by a special Order in Council (collo-
quially known as ''The 'Port to Port' Ordinance,'') for ship's masters to sail with ''sealed
orders,'' or to discharge their cargoes elsewhere
than at the ports specified on the ship's papers.
Other nations had followed the lead, and the German Government instituted a vigilant surveillance
of charters, a sort of charter parties' censorship
which is in vogue to this day.

The weeks passed without further news of the
ship, and T. B. was beginning to worry, for good
reasons. He had an elaborate chart supplied to
him by the Admiralty, which showed him from
day to day, the amount of provisions and coal such
a ship as the *Maria Braganza* would require, and
he knew that she must be running short.

Then came news from Paris that trace of Silinski had been found; and, although the scent was
old, T. B. crossed the Channel the day the message
came.

*   *   *   *

The night of the 1st of March saw T. B. Smith
in Paris. He stayed at the Hotel D'Antin in the
Rue D'Antin, one of those cosy little hostels in
which Paris abounds. His visit was partially successful. He had been able to find traces of Silinski
and his sister; he found their lodgings without
much difficulty. He found, with the aid of a French
detective, the café affected by the precious pair,
and in one way or another was able to collect
quite a considerable amount of useful information
regarding the Silinskis. He was idling away an
evening, sitting before the Café de la Paix, watching the ceaseless procession of people passing to
and fro. This was a favourite amusement of his;
indeed, is it not of every Englishman who finds
himself in Paris with time on his hands?

As he sat there sipping his coffee, a man left
the pavement; and, pulling a chair towards the
next table, seated himself. He was a thick-set man
with a straggling beard, and there was little to
distinguish him from the ordinary citizen. T. B.
gave him a glance and resumed his survey of the

passing crowd. By and by, his attention was again attracted to the neighbouring table by the arrival of another man equally undistinguished. The two men apparently knew one another, for, after a curt meeting, they plunged into a conversation, which was carried on in such low tones that no word reached the detective.

Now, if T. B. had not been a born policeman, he would have been a born journalist, for his ruling passion was an intense curiosity. For aught that he knew, these two might have been engaged in the discussion of some private business matter; the subject of their conversation might indeed have had reference to some intimate family secret. But no sooner had these two very ordinary citizens given evidence of their wish for privacy, than T. B. was overpowered with a desire to act the eavesdropper.

But his unpardonable curiosity was unrewarded save that, by one expression which reached him, he gathered that the conversation was either in Low German or Flemish.

"Mumble, mumble, mumble, mumble," said one rapidly.

"Soh!" said the other nodding.

"Mumble, mumble, mumble, mumble."

"Ja," said the other, and added something in a lower tone.

T. B. was annoyed, not with himself that he should be acting the spy on apparently innocent people; he had no conscience in the matter—but because of the extraordinary and unnecessary care these people were taking to keep their affairs to themselves.

He had a good working knowledge of Flemish —which is Cape Dutch with variations—and he was in a position to understand anything they might say, if they would only have the grace to say it aloud.

At last he gave up his attempt at hearing, in disgust, and opening the *Journal du Soir,* began to read a particularly lurid story of an Apache murder in the Montmartre.

"Mumble, mumble, mumble, mumble," went on the voices; and T. B., in his unjustifiable annoyance, thought twice about the advisability of changing his seat.

He read the case through, turned over a leaf to a brilliant, if wholly illogical article on one of France's inevitable "situations," and was half way through it; then suddenly he stopped reading, and, though his eyes did not leave the printed page, every nerve in his body awoke to life.

"Mumble, mumble, mumble, Silinski, mumble, ship, mumble." He waited. The voices kept up their monotonous burden.

"Silinski—ship!"

That was all; he heard no other word that gave him further clue to the subject of the conversation, but "Silinski—ship" was enough. By and by, he saw a French detective stroll past, saw the swift and apparently careless scrutiny of the officer, and caught his eye. The sign T. B. gave was imperceptible to any save one acquainted with the universal sign-language of the great police world, but the French detective, seeing T. B. rubbing his right eye as if to keep himself awake, knew that he was required, and walking along to the corner of the Place de l'Opera, waited. T. B. was with him in less than a minute, and rapidly explained. The detective listened. He had noticed the men.

"If Monsieur le Commissaire will return to the café and invent some excuse for detaining them, I will do all that is necessary."

T. B. nodded and returned to the café. The men were settling with the waiter when T. B. returned to his seat, with two or three newspapers he had hurriedly purchased at the corner kiosque as an excuse for his absence.

As they rose, T. B. looked the man with the

beard in the face, and, smiling, nodded.

He saw the gathering frown of suspicion, and said. "M. Herhault, n'est ce que pas?"

"You are mistaken, monsieur,' said the man coldly.

"Pardon," T. B. made haste to say with profound humility, "but I am in error. I thought—"

"Good-night, m'sieur," said the other curtly, and turned to go.

"One moment." T. B. laid his hand on the man's arm. "I cannot allow you to go under a misapprehension; will you be seated whilst I explain how I came to make the mistake?"

"Your explanation is unnecessary," said the man shortly. "I beg you not to detain me."

T. B. with one eye for the promenading crowd, saw the French detective pass.

"I will not detain you, m'sieur," he said, with a slight bow.

The two men turned out of the café. He watched them as they crossed the Place, going in the direction of the Rue de la Paix.

At a distance he followed, and saw them turn into a side street. He quickened his steps; and, as he rounded the corner, he came upon a little group in the deserted street. The two men were surrounded by half a dozen plain clothes officers.

They were expostulating vigorously, and their captors stood impassively by.

As T. B. came up to the group two of the French officers took an arm each of the arrested men, whilst one whistled a cab.

T. B. did not follow to the Commissaire's office. He had told the detective all he had heard, and he was content to leave the matter at that.

He returned to his hotel, and waited. It was near midnight before the French officer came.

"We have searched their lodgings, and can find nothing but a little drawing of the cardinal points of the compass," he said.

"Do they deny knowledge of Silinski?"

The Frenchman shrugged his shoulders.

"They deny nothing; they affirm nothing," he said. "It is unusual for my countrymen in the exultation of arrest to make confessions. But I am placing a spy in the same cell, and to-morrow we may learn something. All that we know at present is that they are Frenchmen, although they are visitors from Brussels, that they have been in this city for a month, and are engaged in no known business."

The next morning brought T. B. no further information. The men had remained dumb in the presence of the spy.

"I am afraid that unless we get further evidence, we must release them," said the officer who brought the information. "I am with you in believing that these two men are, or have been, agents of Silinski; but we need a stronger case."

That stronger case did not materialize, and that same night T. B. was informed that the men had been released.

They were carefully watched, but that same night they left by the mail train for Liège.

So much the detective officer related to T. B. over coffee and a cigarette at the Café de la Paix.

"It is very curious," said the French detective thoughtfully; it was La Croix of Lefeu's staff; "that you should have heard them, or one of them, speak of Silinski and a ship. You are sure you were not mistaken?"

T. B. shook his head.

"I do not think you were," said La Croix. "I questioned them and they denied that they knew any such person, or that they had ever mentioned his name. That in itself is suspicious."

"You found nothing in their lodgings?"

"Nothing—except the compass points."

He felt in his breast pocket, took out a notebook, opened it, and extracted a folded sheet of paper. This he smoothed on the marble-topped

table at which they sat. There was no word of
writing on it, only a simple diagram. It was a
cross with tiny circles at the end of each arm, and
a larger circle in the centre.

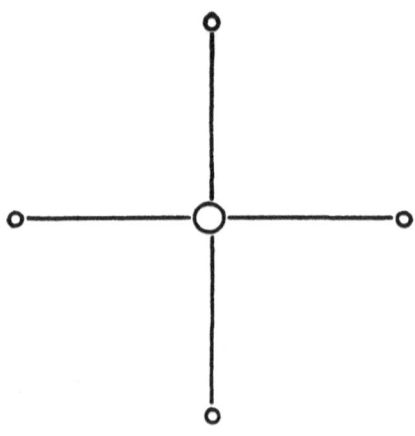

T. B.'s frown spoke eloquently his disappointment.

"This," bantered La Croix, "gives you no clue
to this mysterious 'Lolo' of yours, I suppose?"

T. B. shook his head.

"Does it you?" he asked, and the Frenchman
laughed.

"No," he said, "to me it is only a curious little
cross with no significance."

T. B. smoothed the paper again, and pursed his lips in thought.

"Can I have this?" he demanded after a little while.

"You may have a photograph of it," said the cautious La Croix. "These documents, even the least of them, have some value, and are part of the *dossier;* until we know enough to be able to distinguish between those that count and those that have no bearing whatever on the case, we cannot destroy any of them, or part with them. As it happens, I have anticipated your wishes, for a photograph has already been taken and will be in your possession to-day."

It was the 9th of March when T. B., with the meagre evidence he had been able to secure, together with the unpromising photograph of the meaningless cross, drove down the Gare du Nord on his way back to town. The train was on the point of drawing out when a man came racing along the platform. T. B.'s carriage had been reserved, so that the man had no difficulty in discovering it. He jumped up on the footboard, and thrust a bulky blue package into T. B.'s hand.

"I am from the Chief of the Police," he said breathlessly; "this telegram is for you, and has just arrived."

T. B. thanked him, and the train began to move.

Leaning back amidst the cushions, he unfolded the blue sheets, and read.

The telegram was from Scotland Yard, and began:—

"Officer commanding Gibraltar reports that his wireless station had been intercepting messages in code which bear some resemblance to those of N. H. C. Full messages have been forwarded here for decoding. Some of them are unintelligible, but one portion of a message we have been able to make read: '. . . Accept your assurance and explanation; we have will splendid field for enterprise; I will join you at Lolo with shipload of provisions and collier on June 1st. In meantime, if you do as I suggest we can make terms with Governments and, moreover, find employment agents who are at present discontented . . .' Message beyond this undecipherable with exception of words 'destruction,' 'easily obtainable,' and 'insure.' This message obviously between Silinski and *Maria Braganza*"— Stop. 'Commander Fleet, Gibraltar, has sent H.M.S. *Duncan, Essex, Kent,* with six destroyers into Atlantic pick up *Maria Braganza.* Return immediately.—COMMIS-SIONER."

T. B. read the message again, folded it carefully, and placed it in his breast pocket. There was one word in Silinski's message that revealed in a flash the nature of the new terror with which the Nine Men of Cadiz threatened the world.

CHAPTER XXXII

A MATTER OF INSURANCE

You pass up a broad stone staircase at one end of the Royal Exchange, and come to a landing where, confronting you, are two big swing doors that are constantly opening and closing as bare-headed clerks and top-hatted brokers go swiftly in and out.

On the other side of the doors is a small counter where a man in uniform checks, with keen glance, each passer-by. Beyond the counter are two rooms, one leading to the other, shaped like the letter "L," and in the longer of the two sit in innumerable pews, quiet men with fat notebooks. From desk to desk flutter the brokers bargaining their risks, and there is a quiet but eager buzz of voices through which at intervals booms the stentorian tones of the porter calling by name the members whose presence is required outside.

A stout man made a slow progress down one of the aisles, calling at the little pews *en route,*

270

making notes in a silver-mounted book he held in his hand.

He stopped before the pew of one of the biggest underwriters. *"Taglan Castle?"* he said laconically, and the underwriter looked up over his spectacles, then down at the slip of paper the man put before him.

"One per cent.?" he asked, in some surprise, and the other nodded.

"How much?" he asked.

The underwriter tapped the slip of paper before him.

"Ten thousand pounds at 5s. per centum," he said. "I can do that." He initialled the slip and the man passed on.

He went the round of the room, stopped to exchange a joke with an acquaintance, then descended the stone stairs.

Back to his stuffy little office went the broker with little thought that he had been engaged in any unusual variety of business. In his private room he found his client; a thick-set man with a straggling beard, who rose politely as the broker entered, and removed the cigar he had been smoking.

"You have finish," he said with a slightly foreign accent, and the broker smiled.

"Oh, yes!"—a little pompously, after the manner of all Lloyd's brokers— "no difficulty about the *Taglan,* you know. Mail ship, new steamer, no risks practically on the Cape route; rather a bad business for you; you'll lose your premium."

He shook his head with a show of melancholy, and took a pinch of snuff.

"I have a dream," said the foreigner hastily, "ver' bad dream. I have belief in dreams."

"I daresay," said the broker indulgently. "A sister of mine used to have 'em, or said she had; dreamt a tiger bit her, and sure enough next day she lost her brooch."

He sat at his desk, signed a receipt, counted some notes, and locked them in his drawer.

"You won't get your policies for a day or so," he said; "you're staying——"

"At the Hotel Belgique," said the client, and, pocketing his receipts, he rose.

"Good-day," said the broker, and opened the door.

With a slight bow his client departed, and reached the street.

There was a taxicab drawn up before the door, and two or three gentlemen standing on the pavement before the office.

"Cab, sir?" said the driver, but the foreigner shook his head.

"I think you had better," said a voice in French, and a strong hand grasped his arm.

Before he realized what had happened, the Frenchman was hustled into the cab, two men jumped in with him, the door banged, and the car whirled westward.

It was a car which had extraordinary privileges, for at a nod from the man who sat by the side of the driver, the City police held up the traffic to allow it to pass. It flew down Queen Victoria Street at a much greater speed than is permissible within the City boundaries, and the gloved hands of the policemen on duty at the end of Blackfriars Bridge made a clear way for it.

It turned into Scotland Yard, remained a few minutes, then returned along the Embankment, up Northumberland Avenue, and through a side thoroughfare, to Bow Street.

Thereafter, the Frenchman's experience was bewildering. He was searched, hurried through a passage to a small court where a benevolent-looking gentleman sat behind a table, on a raised dais.

The prisoner was placed in a steel pen, and a quietly-dressed man rose from the solicitors' table, and made a brief statement.

"We shall charge this man with being a suspected person, your worship," he said, "and ask for a remand."

Then another man went into the witness-box.

"My name is Detective-Sergeant Kiegnell, of 'A' Division," he said; "and from information received, I went to 976, Throgmorton Street, where I saw the prisoner. I told him I was a police officer, and should take him into custody."

That was all.

The magistrate scribbled something on a paper before him, and said briefly, "Remanded."

Before the prisoner could say a word, or utter anything more than a *"Sacré!"* he was beckoned from the dock and disappeared from court.

So unimportant was this case that none of the reporters in court troubled to record more than the fact that "a well-dressed man of foreign appearance was charged with loitering with intent."

Certainly nobody associated his arrest with the announcement that the *Taglan Castle* had left Cape Town, homeward bound.

It was an interesting voyage for the passengers of the *Taglan Castle*, which, by the way, carried specie to the amount of £600,000. She left Cape Town soon after dusk. The next morning, to the surprise of her Captain, he fell in with a little

British fleet— the *Doris,* the *Philomel,* and the *St. George,* flying a Commodore's flag.

Greatest surprise of all came to the Captain of the *Taglan Castle* when he received the following signal:

"Slow down to thirteen knots, and do not part company."

To the Captain's "I am carrying the mails," came the laconic message, "I know."

For ten days the four ships kept together, then came the sensation of the voyage. At dawn of the tenth day, a big steamer came into view over the horizon. She was in the direct path of the flotilla and to all appearance she was stationary. Those who were on deck at that early hour, heard shrill bugle sounds from the escorting warships, then suddenly the engine of the *Taglan* stopped, and a crowd of curious passengers came running up from below. The *Taglan Castle* had obeyed a peremptory order given by the *St. George,* and was hove-to.

The *St. George* and *Doris* went on; then from the funnels of the stationary steamer came clouds of smoke, and through their telescope the passengers saw her turn slowly and move.

Slowly, slowly, she got under way, then—

"Bang!"

The forward 9.2 gun of the *St. George* emitted a thin straight streak of flame, and there was a strange whining noise in the air.

"Bang! Bang!"

The *Doris* came into action at the same time as the *St. George* fired her second gun. Both shots fell short, and the spray of the *ricochets* leapt up into the air.

The fugitive steamer was now moving at full speed; there was a great fan-shaped patch of white water at her stern.

"Bang!"

All this time the two British warships were going ahead firing as they went. Then from the stern of the strange steamer floated a whiff of white smoke, and, in a second, the eerie whine of a shell came to the passengers who crowded the deck of the *Taglan Castle*. The shell missed the firing warships; indeed, it did not seem to be aimed in their direction, but it fell uncomfortably close to the mail boat. Another shell fell wide of the steamer but in a line with her. The manœuvre of the flying vessel was now apparent. She carried heavier metal than the second-class cruisers of the British fleet, but her object was to disable the mail boat.

The Captain of the *Taglan* did not wait for

orders; he rung his engines full speed ahead, and swung his helm hard aport. He was going to steam back out of range.

But no further shot came from the *Maria Braganza.*

Smaller and smaller she grew until a pall of smoke on the horizon showed where she lay.

Obeying a signal from the distant warship, the *Taglan* came round again, and in half an hour had come abreast of the two warships, the faithful *Philomel* in attendance.

There was a swift exchange of signals between the warships, and their semaphore arms whirled furiously.

Then the Commodore's ship signalled.

"Hope you are not alarmed; you will not be troubled again; go ahead."

On the twelfth day there was another shock for the excited passengers of the *Taglan Castle,* for, nearing Cape Verde Islands, they came upon not one warship but six—six big black hulls lying at regular intervals along the horizon. But there was no cause for alarm. They were the six Dreadnought cruisers that had been sent down from Gibraltar to take up the burden of the Cape Fleet.

It was all a mystery to the bewildered passengers, whatever it might be to the officers of the

Taglan, who had received a long "lamp" message in the middle of the night.

There was a two hours' delay whilst the Captain of the *St. George* went on board the *Indefatigable* to report.

This was the end of the adventures that awaited the *Taglan.* She was escorted to the Needles by the six warships, and came into Southampton, her passengers a-flutter with that excitement peculiar to men who have come through a great danger, and are exhilarated to find themselves alive.

The arrival of the *Taglan* was opportune; it gave confirmation to the rumours which had been in circulation, and synchronized with the issue of the manifesto of the Nine Men—a manifesto unique in history.

CHAPTER XXXIII

THE MAD WARSHIP

The manifesto had arrived simultaneously at every newspaper office in London, Paris, and Berlin.

"It was printed," says the official record of the incident, with its cold precision and its passion for detail, "on paper of a texture and quality which is generally in use in small Continental newspaper offices. From certain peculiarities of the printed characters, it was seen that the type from which it was printed must have been cast in Spain. Wherever the letter W occurred it was replaced by VV ... The manifesto was neatly folded and enclosed in an envelope of octavo size, and the actual sheet-size was what is known in the printing trade as double-crown. The postage stamps were Spanish, the place of posting, as revealed by the office post-marks, were in some cases Malaga, and in some, Algeciras. The fact that, whether posted at one place or the other the date

of the posting was identical, supports the view
that at least two persons had been concerned in
the dispatch.''

The manifesto itself ran:—

''TO THE CIVILIZED NATION (*sic*).

''Whereas, we, the company known âs the Nine
Men of Cadiz, have been placed by universal decree outside the law, and whereas it is against our
desires that such decrees of outlawry should exist
against us, both from the point of view of our own
personal comfort and safety, and from the point
of view of the free exchange of commercial (*sic*)
relationships.

''Now, therefore, we decree—

''That unless an immediate free pardon be
granted to each and every man on board the *Maria
Braganza* and liberty be given to him to go his
way peaceably without arrest or fear of molesta-
tions (*sic*), the owners and crew of the *Maria
Braganza* will declare war upon the commerce of
the world. It will loot and destroy such shipping
as may with advantage be so looted and destroyed,
and in the end will fight to the last against its
aggressor.

''(Signed) By order of the Nine,

''SILINSKI.''

It is no exaggeration to say that the publication of this manifesto caused a panic, not only in shipping circles, but throughout the civilized world. The sea held a hidden danger, neither life nor property were secure. There came to stay-at-home people a realization of the dependence of these islands upon its oversea trade. That insurance rates should rise was only a natural and immaterial result of the publication of the threat. But a more serious aspect was the instant effect the manifesto had upon the grain market. Bread rose in two days from 4d. to 6d., and, in some parts of the country 7d., a loaf.

That the fears of the community were justified was proved by the story of the *Taglan Castle,* and was proved beyond doubt two days after the publishing of the Nine Men's proclamation by what happened to the *Zeider Prince,* a Welsh collier bound from Cardiff to Valparaiso. The port authorities at St. Vincent (Teneriffe) reported that heavy cannonading had been heard by the coastguards on the western shore of the island. The firing lasted three minutes and then ceased. Fortunately, there was in the harbour of St. Vincent at the time, the British destroyer *Alert,* which, on receipt of the news, went out at full speed to investigate. The *Alert* came up to the scene of the crime after the *Zeider Prince* had been sunk (a lifebuoy and a waterlogged boat were taken on board the destroyer to establish the identity of the doomed ship).

When the *Alert* came up, the *Maria Braganza* was hull down, and steaming due west, and the Captain of the destroyer very pluckily gave chase. With the *Alert's* enormous speed she overhauled the battleship hand over hand, but long before she could get within striking distance, the *Maria Braganza* opened fire on her, and it was only by a miracle that the *Alert* escaped destruction. The destroyer had neither the coal nor the stores necessary for a long chase, and returned to Teneriffe.

The theory in regard to the *Zeider Prince* is that she was first brought alongside the battleship, her cargo taken aboard, and then the little tramp was sunk. No member of her crew was found, dead or alive, and the assumption at the time was that the crew were prisoners on board the warship— an assumption which afterwards proved to be accurate.

Less fortunate were the men who manned the German steamer *Aosan Werthan,* bound from Hamburg to the ivory coast with a general cargo. The dead body of a sailor washed up near Cape Blanca was the first intimation of the tragedy.

It was the only intimation, for from that day to this no word has ever reached the world of its fate.

There was consternation enough at these events, but within a fortnight came the story of the North Atlantic outrage.

The *Caratana*, the fastest mail-ship afloat, as well as being nearly the largest, was sixty hours out of New York with 350 passengers on board, when she came up with a strange warship flying a red flag. The warship hoisted an unintelligible signal, which the Captain of the *Caratana* did not understand. It was followed by one of which there could be no mistaking the meaning.

"Stop, or I will sink you."

The Captain of the Atlantic liner knew all that was known about the *Maria Braganza,* and at once realized his danger. If he did not realize it, there came a shell from the warship, which passed astern. Fortunately, there was a mist on the water which grew in density every minute—a real "bank" fog, not usually met with so far east.

The Captain of the *Caratana* decided upon the course of action he would take. Very quickly he signalled "I surrender," and rang his engines to "stop." The men on the warship seemed satisfied with his action, and no further demonstration was made against the liner. Such was the "way" on

the big ship, that although her propellers had
ceased to revolve, she continued her course, nearer
and nearer she grew to a thick patch of fog that
lay ahead of her. The *Maria Braganza* may have
suspected the manœuvre, for she signalled, "Go
astern."

For answer, the Captain of the *Caratana* put
port and starboard engine full ahead, and, whilst
men were running to their stations on the warship,
the *Caratana* slipped into the fog belt.

In an instant the *Maria Braganza* was blotted
from view.

The liner Captain put his helm over to starboard, and it was well that he did so, for with a
reverberating crash, the warship opened fire in
the direction he had disappeared. Shell after shell
came flying through the thick mist, and the thud of
their impact as they struck the water came to the
ears of the affrighted passengers.

The sound of spasmodic firing grew fainter and
fainter every minute as the great steamer went
threshing through the swirling fog, until it ceased
altogether.

Although no harm had befallen the liner, the
news of the attack produced a profound sensation.
Its effect was to paralyse the business of ocean
travel. "The Mad Warship" terrorized the seas.

Immediately intelligence of the outrage was flashed by wireless telegraphy to America, the American Fleet, which had been cruising up the Atlantic coast, steamed out to intercept the *Maria Braganza;* and, simultaneously, the Home Fleet, which was lying in Queenstown Harbour, sailed to meet them. The American Fleet consisted of the battleships *New Jersey, Connecticut, Idaho,* and *Michigan;* the armoured cruisers *St. Louis* and *Maryland;* and the protected cruisers *Salem, Chattanooga, Olympia,* and *Tacoma.* The cruisers went on, and two and a half days later came up with the *Warrior, Achilles, Invincible* and *Indomitable,* of the British Fleet.

But no sign had they seen of the *Maria Braganza,* which must have headed due south.

It was on the day the report of their non-success reached England that T. B. Smith located Silinski.

*   *   *   *

There languished in a prosaic prison cell at Brixton gaol a Monsieur Torquet, who was admittedly a victim of a police persecution. That much I think T. B. himself was prepared to admit. He had come before a police magistrate; had been remanded and again remanded; he had communicated first with the Belgian Ambassador, who found it convenient to disown him as a Belgian;

he had applied to the French Consul, and that gentleman had replied to the communication with a promptitude and a finality which suggest that the whole of the circumstances of the case had been in the possession of the Consulate, and the application anticipated.

This, indeed, was the fact.

M. Torquet was suspected not of a crime against any particular section of society, but indeed of being accessory to a crime against humanity; and T. B. was prepared to run a tilt at the very Habeas Corpus Act rather than release his grip upon the stranger with the straggling beard, whom he had recognized as being the mumbling gentleman of the Café de la Paix, who knew of Silinski and of "ships"; and, knowing so much about the latter, had heavily insured the *Taglan Castle* before she started out on her adventurous voyage.

So, through the days of the terror, M. Torquet was a prisoner in Brixton, watched day and night, taking his exercise aloof and at separate hours from the other prisoners; and, moreover, denied the satisfaction of knowing that public interest was excited in his fate.

For nobody knew of M. Torquet. The most astute reporters who had seen the thick-set figure stumble up the steps of the dock in the Extradition Court had failed to connect him with the subject that was filling every mind, and, incidentally, every available column in the newspapers. It is a fact that all through the period of incarceration no man had attempted by threat, entreaty, or promise, to extract from him the secret he undoubtedly held.

The police had waited for a voluntary statement; they applied to him the supreme torture of indifference.

Day by day men had brought him food, warders who were apparently dumb had led him forth to the paved exercise yard, and had led him back again. He had been kept supplied with books and writing materials, the food that came to him was well cooked, every consideration was shown to him; but nobody displayed any desire to share his confidence, or to be interested in any way in him, save as a rare animal to be fed and exercised.

He had been remanded and remanded. Finally, he had been committed for trial.

It does not seem possible that evidence could be produced in open court—evidence sufficient to constitute a *primâ facie* case for trial—without the event being reported, yet this was what happened.

Into the Extradition Court at Bow Street, generally supposed to be closed for the day, the man

was hurried. A magistrate took his seat on the
bench, evidence was given—there were two police
witnesses—the committal was signed, and before
the faintest rumour reached the general court that
the other court was open, before a reporter could
gather up his block and pad and hurry out, the
sitting was completed, and no man was wiser.

This M. Torquet, brooding in the loneliness of
his cell at Brixton, had very nearly reached the
limits of his patience; the silence and the indifference had crushed what little there was in him.

For two months he had lain without trial, in a
cell which had a table on which were pen, paper,
and ink. He had not in all that time touched the
one or the other, but on the day that the Atlantic
liner came across the *Maria Braganza* he sat at the
table and wrote a brief note to the governor of
the prison. Within an hour T. B. Smith was ushered into the cell and remained with the man for
some time. Then he came out and sent for a short-
hand clerk, and together they returned.

For four hours the three men worked, one ques-
tioning and translating, one answering, at first
sullenly and with periodic outbursts of temper,
and later eagerly, volubly—and all this time the
clerk wrote and wrote, until one notebook was
exhausted and he sent out for another.

It was late in the evening when he said:

"And that, monsieur, is all."

"All?" T. B.'s eyebrows rose. "All? But you have not explained the whereabouts of Lolo?"

The prisoner was frankly puzzled.

"Lolo?" he repeated. "M'sieur, I do not understand."

It was T. B.'s turn to be astonished.

"But the rendezvous—there was to be some rendezvous where the ship would come to pick up any member of the Nine who might become detached."

The man shook his head, and at that moment an idea occurred to T. B. He drew from his pocket a copy of the little "cross with the nobs," as it had been named at Scotland Yard.

"Do you know this?" he asked.

The man looked at it, and smiled.

"Yes—Silinski drew that for me on the last occasion I met him in Paris."

"What does it mean?"

Again the prisoner shook his head.

"I do not know," he said simply. "Silinski was telling me something of his plans. He drew the cross and was beginning to explain its meaning and then for some reason he stopped, crumpled up the paper, and threw it into the fireplace. At the time I attached some importance to it, and after he had gone I rescued it, but——''

''You don't understand it?''

''I don't,'' said the man, and T. B. knew that he spoke the truth.

CHAPTER XXXIV

IN TANGIER

Many little houses are on the Marshan, the plateau that commands Tangier. They are villas in which Moorish, Spanish, and English styles of architecture, struggling for supremacy, have compromised in a conglomerate type. In one of these houses lived Gregory Silinski and his sister. There is every excuse for a rich Madrid merchant taking up his residence in this pleasant land, more especially in the spring, most especially when the rich Madrid merchant is an invalid. This was Silinski's *rôle* for the moment.

Like most people of the Polish race, he had an aptitude for languages, and his Arabic was well-night faultless.

The man had a passion for organization, and in an incredibly short space of time he had created a secret service of his own.

In Tangier, the very centre of international intrigue, where the Embassies beamed at one another over the dinner table, and plotted their host's ruin in the dark of the night, Silinski might be sure that if his presence in Tangier excited any comment, it would be of a harmless character to himself. Each Embassy would write him down as the agent of the other.

Silinski found the African city a convenient hiding place for many reasons, and was content to remain in his pleasant villa overlooking the Straits, until the *Maria Braganza* forced from a reluctant Europe pardon on her own terms.

It is well to mention that Catherine Silinski shared neither the patience nor the optimism of her brother.

Catherine Silinski must pay the penalty of being her brother's sister. It has been suggested that she is worthy of a whole biography to herself, but such particulars as I have been able to secure of her life do not support this view. Had Catherine lived up to her excommunication—for she once fell under the ban of Holy Church—she might have been great; had she rivalled her brother in villainy, she would have merited the respectful notice of criminologists. As it was, she excites the curiosity only of that section of the morbid and unlettered public which finds more gloomy pleasure in surveying the instrument with which a crime is committed, than in the psychology which enables the thoughtful student to appreciate the criminal's state of mind before the deed.

I believe that she had no moral sense; that she was one of those strange creatures without love or fear. I cannot think that even for her brother she entertained the slightest spark of affection. An accident of nature had made them interdependent; circumstances had thrown them together more than either of them could have desired.

Catherine was by nature luxurious. Adventure separable from comfort she had no heart in. As agent, and well-paid agent, of the Nine Men, she had come to London, and gladly accepted the music-hall engagement for which her talent fitted her.

She was prepared to work adventure within adventure, to let private enterprise run with larger schemings.

Then, of a sudden, the ground had been cut from underneath her feet, first by an urbane detective who had shipped her whither she had no desire to go, secondly by the disappearance of the golden source of her comfort.

Nor was Silinski himself in much better case. He had sufficient money at hand to take him to the West Indies once he was clear of Spain.

He went to Jamaica because, frugal soul that

he was, he discovered that it was almost as cheap to go in person, as it would be to cable—and much safer. Then, he thought, Catherine would have money with her, or the means of getting it.

When they had paid their fares back to England —Silinski affected a little beard in those troublous days—they exhausted their stock of ready money.

It must have been whilst Silinski was in Paris that the ruling spirit of the *Maria Braganza* discovered that Silinski was indispensable, and that strange reconciliation occurred. Through what agency Baggin and he came into touch is not known. It is generally supposed that the warship ventured close to the French or Spanish coast and sent a message of good-will flickering through space, and that some receiving station, undiscovered and undemolished—there must have been a score of such stations—received it, and transmitted it to Silinski. At any rate, it would appear that Silinski became suddenly affluent, and that he was—in Tangier—reputed wealthy.

For this accession to comfort I find an explanation, more simple than that offered by the majority of biographers of the "Nine Men of Cadiz." There can be little doubt, that, by one of those extraordinary coincidences which no writer of fiction could dare fabricate, Silinski had met the sec-

ond Brazilian sailor—that Alverez who was "not
of great mentality and preferred Paris," and had
succeeded in securing no small amount of the ex-
quartermaster's money.

But to return to Catherine Silinski.

I reconstruct the scene when Catherine deliv-
ered her ultimatum—Catherine grown weary of
waiting, grown tired with forced seclusion; Catherine divorced of an admiring audience, and being
moreover a recipient of daily doles, for as I have
explained Silinski was a careful man where money
was concerned.

They sat on either side of a table in the spacious
living-room of their villa. The night was unusually warm, and the French windows were open, but
the jalousies were closed.

The room in which they sat was well furnished
for Silinski was a man of some taste.

He himself was engaged in making notes in a
large exercise book, and Catherine was pretending
to read. From time to time she glanced across the
table at him, but he did not look up. Once, her
glance rested longer than usual, and he might have
seen that look of calm dispassionate speculation
which was the peculiar possession of the Silinski
family—a cold appraisement.

When she spoke it was patiently and quietly.

"Gregory," she said suddenly, "how does this end?"

"This?" He looked up enquiringly.

"This," she repeated. "This hiding and seeking; these mysteries—and poverty?"

He smiled gently, and shook his head as one reluctant to reprove, but compelled by circumstances to administer a chiding.

"Poverty, as the great Cervantes once said ——" he began.

"I would rather not discuss Cervantes," she interrupted coolly. "I do not know who Cervantes was, though there was a little man in Madrid who showed me a great deal of attention, who had that name. Gregory, what is the end of this, for me, and you?"

He stroked his moustache with caressing white fingers.

"Wealth," he said, after a while, "enormous wealth; our share of the profits we secured for our friends of Cadiz. It will not be difficult to reach the *Maria Braganza*. It will be less difficult to leave her when our share has been apportioned. More than our share," he added, thoughtfully, "for there is a man on that ship with whom I have some score to settle."

She made no answer, but absently fingered the paper of her book.

"You are once more in touch with them?" she asked, and Silinski nodded.

"How?"

He smiled. He loved a mystery, yet there was no mystery in the matter. In the days before the Nine Men had been scattered, Silinski had foreseen the necessity for establishing wireless stations that would be, because of their very openness, free from suspicion. He had no difficulty in persuading the young Sultan, Abdul Asziz, to grant a concession empowering the erection of experimental wireless stations, for Abdul Asziz dearly loved a toy, greatly desired, too, amongst Europeans the reputation of being a progressive monarch. So that the high masts of the Anglo-Sevilla Wireless Company stood by the lighthouse, at Cape Spartel, and had so stood for two years. When the hasty inspection of existing stations had been made by the powers, the Cape Spartel installation had not been suspected, and Silinski's agents had been permitted to continue their experiments. It was a simple explanation; it explained in fact Silinski's presence in Tangier, but he did not feel disposed to offer it.

So his cryptic smile was all the answer that Catherine received.

"Is there not a reward for the arrest of the Nine Men?" she asked.

"There is, my child," he replied.

"And a pardon?"

"And a pardon."

She was silent and sat with her eyes fixed on the table.

"A reward of ten thousand pounds?" she repeated. "How much is that?"

"A little more than a quarter of a million francs. Why do you ask?"

He looked at her keenly as he spoke, searching her every feature as though he would surprise a secret.

"Why do you not take the reward?" she said calmly, and he stifled a little sigh of relief.

"Because, my dear Catherine, I am what these English call a party to the crime—and in the amiable proclamation which the English Government issued a short time since, I was specifically named."

She was silent for such a long time, that he had resumed his work. Then—

"What will they do to you, if they capture

you?" she asked, and he laid down his pen again, with an exaggerated air of patience.

"They will hang me by the neck until I am dead," he said, and Catherine did not shudder, as a thousand other women would have done, but nodded.

"And me?"

"You, my dear Catherine?" Silinski looked at her again, with swift suspicion. "You? I think because of your youth and beauty, but more because you are not as deeply involved as the rest of us, you might escape with a few years' imprisonment—let us say seven."

"I see."

She took up her book again, and idly turned the leaves. "Seven years is a long time," she commented reflectively.

"Eternity is longer," said Silinski.

Catherine did not answer. She was apparently interested in her book, and Silinski, after waiting for her to speak, took up his pen again.

He worked steadily for two hours, during which time Catherine made no further attempts to speak.

He finished his work, read it over carefully, blotted the book, and rose.

He pushed open the jalousies and stepped into the little garden. From the villa, a hill sloped downward to the town. It was a calm moonlight night, and the crude white of Tangier was softened in the silver beams. There were many twinkling lights in the town, and the bay was laced with light.

He walked through the garden, and moved toward the sea.

From where he stood he could not distinguish the little ship that lay under steam round the shoulder of the cliff. A tiny Spanish steamer that wandered from port to port, from Casa Blanca to Ceutra, from Tangier to Mogador, carrying passengers in the tourist season, and cargo all the year round. Silinski had a "friend" in command of the *Doro*. The fact that he was a friend of Silinski's is sufficient to indicate that he was none of Nature's noblemen, and I say this in no uncharity. It was rumoured in Gibraltar that the *Doro* had been engaged in not a few gun-running adventures on the Moorish coast, and on one occasion there had been a Court of Inquiry following upon a seizure, but nothing had come of that.

Silinski walked back to the villa, and stood for a time on the white road that led past the house, his head on one side, absorbing the beauty of the scene—for there was poetry in the man.

Then he walked slowly to the house.

Catherine was sitting as he had left her, the book—it was one of Guadilva's romances, and bore a gaudy picture on its cover—before her. She too had been thinking, for Silinski noted that the page was open at the identical illustration he had seen when he went out.

He took up his work where he left off, opened his little book, unscrewed his stylographic pen, and began to work.

Suddenly he stopped and, looking up, caught his sister's eyes fixed upon him.

"My friend," he said, picking up the conversation where they had dropped it, "you worry too much about things that do not concern you."

She shrugged her shoulders.

"I think seven years' imprisonment concerns me very much," she said. "I should be an old woman at the end of that time."

"It will never come to that," said Silinski sharply—for him. "You seem to think we shall fail. Do you not realize that we are on the verge of our greatest success?"

She smiled, a little scornfully.

"Men are always on the verge of success who end their lives in failure," she said. "There is no verge to real success; it opens under you and you fall into it."

"You are too clever," said Silinski. "You have read that somewhere. After all," he went on, "you have less to fear than most of us; and you forget that you are only a very small piece in the game."

Then he made a mistake, a bad mistake for a man of his finesse.

"We will find you a husband, Catherine," he said, with humour. "It shall be Baggin or Meyers —somebody immensely rich, and you shall live on a beautiful island, and have thousands of slaves."

All the time she was looking at him thoughtfully.

She nodded slightly when he finished, and went on reading.

Silinski retired that night just before there came floating up from the town below the voice of the muezzin calling the faithful to prayer. He slept on the ground floor, and he was dozing when there was a tapping on his window pane.

He got up and opened the window, for he recognized an agent from the wireless station.

"Senor," whispered the man, "have you heard the news?"

"No; what is it?"

"Monsieur Zillier has escaped from Devil's Island—the news came across from Gibraltar to-night.''

"Are you sure?" whispered Silinski, eagerly.

For answer the man produced a slip of paper.

Silinski took it, closed the shutters, and turned on the electric light.

The paper, crumpled and soiled, was a copy of the garrison orders of Gibraltar, and under the routine duties appeared the ''News of the Day.''

Yes, there it was.

''The man Zillier, convicted in connection with the Nine Men of Cadiz conspiracy, has escaped from Devil's Island.''

That was all.

Silinski read it again, then he extinguished the lights, and reopened the window.

''Take this,'' he said, handing the paper to the man. ''All night call the Nine, and if you get an answer convey the news to them. They must know, for Zillier will endeavour to reach the rendezvous on June the first.''

After the man had gone, he returned to bed, and lay staring into the darkness. If Zillier joined the *Maria Braganza,* he must join it also; that much he decided. And Catherine—? He frowned. Catherine was getting a little difficult to manage.

Before he fell asleep he decided to cut himself adrift from her. Curiously enough some such resolution had already been made by Catherine.

      *   *   *   *

Three days later Silinski returned from a walk in the best of humours. He had been out to the station near Cape Spartel. After two days the operators had got into communication with the *Maria Braganza,* and the news was satisfactory.

He burst in upon Catherine as she was settling herself down for a siesta.

"Catherine, my child," he said, with a gesture that was peculiarly his, "soon you are to lose your unsympathetic brother, my little one; yet be assured that his thoughts will ever be with you, his eyes tearful——"

"And what does all this mean?" she added, very wakeful indeed now.

He waved his hands airily.

"A little separation," he said. "I must go to meet the Nine Men; after a while I shall, of course, return——"

"But what of me?" she said. "Do I stay in this town of dogs and smells? Do I bury myself in Tangier and grow old?"

"I will leave you money," he said. "I have

made certain arrangements; you will have ten thousand pesetas.''

She laughed.

''Ten thousand pesetas!'' she scoffed; ''to last me for eternity!''

''Madame,'' he said gravely—Silinski was unusually impressive when he was grave—''I shall return.''

She made a little grimace, was about to speak, then shut her mouth tightly as though to check something that were better not said.

''When do you purpose leaving?'' she asked.

''To-morrow—the next day—who knows?'' he answered vaguely. ''There are many things to do. The English Government have become interested in the wireless station. They have been putting on foot inquiries, which are not likely to allay any suspicion we have aroused. It would be better if some of our instruments were dismantled and taken away; they will be difficult to replace.''

He rattled on, giving her, amongst other things, such purely domestic instructions as to the disposal of such of his linen as was still with their Moorish laundry.

To all this she listened patiently, even interposed a few suggestions of her own.

Silinski, prepared for something of a scene at

his bare-face desertion, was relieved, and showed it. He was in an exultant mood throughout that day, hummed such airs as occurred to him, whistled, made little jokes, and went on with his packing for all the world like some everyday clerk released from the bondage of office work to his annual holiday.

Less boisterous was Catherine. She, too, was busy in a quiet way. In the confusion of his packing, Silinski did not notice at first that Catherine was packing also. When he did he dropped the work he was at the moment engaged in, and came to her.

"Beloved," he said seriously, "what are you doing?"

"I am packing," she replied calmly.

"But," he urged gently; "you do not understand. I will return——"

"I shall not be here," she said, without raising her voice. "You did not expect me to stay in this place, did you?"

"At least, you will wait until I have gone?" he asked, ignoring her question. He had only the vaguest interest in her fate thereafter. Indeed, he thought it likely that Catherine might remain at liberty less than a week following his disappearance. You may be sure that Silinski had studied

the situation in all its aspects. He had thought at
first of taking her with him on board the *Maria
Braganza,* but he foresaw complication. Her presence might strengthen his position with the Nine;
at the same time it might easily bring about his
own undoing.

"Have no fear," she answered his question. "I
shall wait for your departure."

. "That might well be," thought Silinski, for he
had timed his departure for that very night. The
Doro waited for him, and the dark of the night
would bring a boat to the shore to take him and his
belongings aboard.

"Where do you meet our friends?" she asked
suddenly.

"At the rendezvous," Silinski answered instantly, "although it is a great secret, little one, I will
tell you; it is a spot on the map nine hundred miles
south of Bermuda, in the midst of a desolation of
water; here will Gregory Silinski, an outlaw, join
his fellow outcasts."

He grew pensive at the melancholy picture he
drew, and sighed.

"Nine hundred miles south of Bermuda," she
repeated absently.

"To be exact," said Silinski carefully, "eight
hundred and ninety-four miles."

She nodded.

"I wonder where the rendezvous really is!" she said with a smile.

"I have told you——"

"You have told me a lie," she interrupted him, still smiling, and Silinski smiled in sympathy.

He made many visits to the wireless station that day. It was a hot and dusty walk, but he regarded neither heat nor discomfort. Late in the afternoon, just as darkness fell, returning to the villa, he found it deserted, save for the two Moorish servants of the house. Their mistress had gone out, so they said, into the town. They had scarcely finished answering the questions that Silinski put to them when Catherine walked in.

"Where have you been?" he asked. He made no pretence at being polite, for he was perturbed in mind.

"To the city," she said coolly.

"Why?"

"To book my passage by the *Petalygo!*"

"Why?"

She made no answer.

"Why?" he asked again.

She shrugged her shoulders.

"Have I not answered? As soon as you have left Tangier, I also leave."

"Why did you go into Tangier?" He was in-
sistent, and she saw she had need for caution.

"I have told you—to book my passage to Cadiz."

He laughed harshly.

"Book your passage to Hades, my friend!" he
said. "You went to Tangier for a purpose."

For answer she turned upon him with a con-
temptuous gesture, and walked quickly to her
room. She heard him follow with quick steps, and
shut the door in his face; before he could grasp
the handle of the door, he heard the key turn in the
lock. He was of a mind to kick in the door, for he
had an instinct for danger, and knew that he was
in deadly peril.

Instead, he knocked at the door gently.

"Catherine," he said softly, "Catherine, little
one; I am sorry I offended you."

There was no answer.

"I was annoyed because you went into Tangier
without telling me. It was indiscreet, my dear.
Open the door and I will explain."

He heard her footsteps on the floor of the room,
and slipped from his hip-pocket the thin-bladed
knife he had found so useful many times before.

But she did not come to the door. He heard a
drawer open, the soft "click" of a Browning

pistol being charged, and replaced his knife with a little grin which meant many things.

He went back to the sitting-room. It was quite dark now, but he did not attempt to turn on the lights.

He sat down to think. His baggage he had sent away during the afternoon. The men would now be waiting for him with the boat, though it was early. He could have wished to settle matters with Catherine. How much did she know? He did not rate the intelligence of women very highly, but Catherine was a Silinski. Yet, remarkably enough, he had never before seriously considered the extent of Catherine's knowledge.

A suspicious man sitting in the dark, rapidly reviewing such a position as this, is not likely to think evenly or justly, and perhaps Silinski overestimated Catherine's astuteness. Be that as it may, he came to a decision.

He stepped softly into the garden, and came to a spot beneath her window.

"Catherine," he called, and he saw her dimly, for there was no light in her room.

She stood a little way back from the open casement, but he judged the distance between himself and her with tolerable precision.

Like a flash, his arm rose, and the thin-bladed

knife went whistling through the air.

He heard a sharp cry; then silence.

He waited a little while, and walked through the garden. There was a man standing in the middle of the white road. His hands in his overcoat pocket, the red glow of his cigar a point of light in the gloom. Farther away, he saw the figures of three horsemen.

"Silinski, I suppose," drawled a voice—the voice of T. B. Smith. "Put up your hands or you're a dead man."

CHAPTER XXXV

SILINSKI LEAVES HURRIEDLY

In an instant the road was filled with men; they must have been crouching in the shadow of the grassy plateau, but in that same instant Silinski had leapt back to the cover of the garden. A revolver banged behind him; and, as he ran, he snatched his own revolver from his pocket, and sent two quick shots into the thick of the surrounding circle. There was another gate at the farther end of the garden; there would be men there, but he must risk it. He was slight and had some speed as a runner; he must depend upon these gifts.

He opened the gate swiftly and sprang out. There were three or four men standing in his path. He shot at one point blank, dodged the others, and ran. He judged that his pursuers would not know the road as well as he. Shot after shot rang out behind him. He was an easy mark on the white road, and he turned aside and took to the grass. He was clear of the houses now, and

312

there was no danger ahead, but the men who followed him were untiring.

Presently, he struck the footpath across the sloping plain that led to the shore, and the going was easier.

It was Silinski's luck that his pursuers should have missed the path. His every arrangement worked smoothly, for the boat was waiting, the men at their oars, and he sprang breathlessly into the stern.

It was a circumstance, which might have struck him as strange, had be been in a condition for calm thought, that the horsemen who were of the party that surrounded him had not joined in pursuit.

But there was another mystery that the night revealed. He had been on board the *Doro* for an hour, and the crew of the little ship was pushing her southward before he went to the cabin that had been made ready for him.

His first act was to take his revolver from his pocket, preparatory to reloading it from the cartridges stored in one of his trunks.

Two chambers of the pistol were undischarged, and, as he jerked back the extractor, these two shells fell on the bed. He looked at them stupidly.

Both cartridges were blank!

*   *   *   *

Had he heard T. B. Smith speaking as he went flying down the road, Silinski might have understood.

"Where's the dead man?" said T. B. cheerfully.

"Here, sir," said a voice.

"Good." Then in Spanish he addressed a figure that stood in the doorway.

"Were you hurt, senora?"

Catherine's little laugh of contempt came out to him.

"I know Gregory," she said quietly; "there is not a trick of his that I have not seen. I was expecting the knife before he raised his arm; has he got safely away?"

"I hope so," said T. B. Then, "You have learnt nothing more?"

"Nothing," she said. "He told me a story of the rendezvous, but it was, of course, a lie; but I have earned my reward."

"I think you need have no fear as to that," said the detective. "Although I knew that your brother was somewhere on this coast, I should, in all probability, have arrived days too late but for your telegram; you will remain in Tangier under the protection of the British Consul."

He was going away, but she called him.

"I cannot understand why you allowed my

brother to escape——" she began. "That you should desire blank cartridges to be placed in his revolver is not so difficult, but I do not see——"

"I suppose not," said T. B. politely, and left her abruptly.

He sprang on to a horse that was waiting, and went clattering down the hill, through the Sôk, down the narrow main street that passes the mosque; dismounting by the Custom House, he placed his horse in charge of a waiting soldier, and walked swiftly along the narrow wooden pier.

At the same time as Silinski was boarding the *Doro,* T. B. was being rowed in a cockleshell of a pinnace to the long destroyer which lay, without lights, in the bay.

He swung himself up a tiny ladder on to the steel deck that rang hollow under his feet.

"All right?" said a voice in the darkness.

"All right," said T. B.; a bell tinkled somewhere, the destroyer moved slowly ahead, and swung out to sea.

"Will you have any difficulty in picking her up?" He was standing in the cramped space of the little bridge, wedged between a quick-firing gun and the navigation desk.

"No—I think not," said the officer; "our difficulty will be to keep out of sight of her. It will be an easy matter to keep her in view because she stands high out of the water, and she is pretty sure to burn her regulation lights. By day I shall let her get hull down and take her masts for guide.''

It was the strangest procession that followed the southern bend of the African Coast. First went the *Doro*, its passengers serenely unconscious of the fact that six miles away, below the rim of the horizon, followed a slim ugly destroyer that did not once lose sight of the *Doro's* mainmast; behind the destroyer, and three miles distant, came six destroyers steaming abreast. Be-. hind them, four miles away, six swift cruisers.

That same night there steamed from Funchal in the Island of Madeira, the *Victor Hugo, Condé, Gloire,* and the *Edgard Quinet* of the French fleet; the *Roon, Yorck, Prinz Adalbert,* and the battleship *Pommern,* of the German navy, with sixteen destroyers, and followed a parallel ocean path.

After three days' steaming, the *Doro* turned sharply to starboard, and the unseen fleets that dogged her turned too. In that circle of death, for a whole week, the little Spanish steamer twisted and turned, and, obedient to the message that went from destroyer to cruiser, the fleets followed her every movement. For the *Doro* was un-

consciously leading the nations to the mad battleship. She had been slipped with that object. So
far every part of the plan had worked well. To
make doubly sure, the news of Zillier's escape
from Devil's Island had been circulated in every
country. It was essential that if they missed the
Maria Braganza this time, they should catch her
on the first of June at "Lolo."

"And where that is," said T. B. in despair,
"heaven only knows."

Wearing a heavy overcoat, he was standing on
the narrow deck of the destroyer as she pounded
through the seas. They had found the South-East
trade winds at a surprisingly northerly latitude,
and the sea was choppy and cold.

Young Marchcourt, the youthful skipper of the
Martine, grinned.

" 'Lolo' is 'nowhere,' isn't it?" he said.
"You'll find it charted on all Admiralty maps; it's
the place where the supply transport is always
waiting on manœuvres—I wish to heaven these
squalls would drop," he added irritably, as a
sudden gust of wind and rain struck the tiny ship.

"Feel sea-sick?" suggested T. B. maliciously.

"Not much—but I'm horribly afraid of losing
sight of this hooker ahead."

He lifted the flexible end of a speaking tube, and pressed a button.

"Give her a few more revolutions, Cole," he said. He hung up the tube. "We look like carrying this weather with us for a few days," he said, "and as I don't feel competent to depend entirely upon my own eyesight, I shall bring up the *Magneto* and the *Solus* to help me watch this beggar."

Obedient to his signal, two destroyers were detached from the following flotilla, and came abreast at dusk.

The weather grew rapidly worse, the squalls of greater frequence. The sea rose, so that life upon the destroyer was anything but pleasant. At midnight, T. B. Smith was awakened from a restless sleep by a figure in gleaming oilskins.

"I say," said a gloomy voice, "we've lost sight of that dashed *Doro*."

"Eh?"

T. B. jumped from his bunk, to be immediately precipitated against the other side of the cabin.

"Lost her light—it has either gone out or been put out. We're going ahead now full speed in the hope of overhauling her——"

Another oil-skinned figure came to the door.

"Light ahead, sir."

"Thank heaven!" said the other fervently, and bolted to the deck.

T. B. struggled into his clothing, and with some difficulty made his way to the bridge. As he climbed the little steel ladder, he heard the engine bell ring, and instantly the rattle and jar of the engines ceased.

"She's stationary," explained the officer, "so we've stopped. She has probably upset herself in this sea."

"How do you know she is stationary?" asked T. B., for the two faint stars ahead told him nothing.

"Got her riding lights," said the other laconically.

Those two riding lights stopped the destroyer; it stopped six other destroyers, far out of sight, six obedient cruisers came to a halt, and a hundred miles or so away, the combined French and German fleets became stationary.

All through the night the watchers lay, heaving, rolling, and pitching, like so many logs on the troubled seas. Dawn broke mistily, but the lights still gleamed. Day came in dull greyness, and the young officer, with his eyes fastened to his binoculars, looked long and earnestly ahead.

"I can see a mast," he said doubtfully, "but

there's something very curious about it."

Then he put down his glasses suddenly, put out his hand, and rang his engines full ahead.

He turned to the quarter-master at his side.

"Get the Commodore by wireless," he said rapidly, "the *Doro* has gone."

Gone, indeed, was the *Doro*—gone six hours since.

They found the lights. They were still burning when the destroyer came up with them.

A roughly built raft with a pole lashed upright, and from this was suspended two lanterns.

Whilst the fleet had watched this raft, the *Doro* had gone on. Nailed to the pole was a letter. It was sodden with spray, but T. B. had no difficulty in reading it.

"*Cher ami,*" it ran, "much as I value the honour of a naval escort, its presence is embarrassing at the moment. I saw your destroyer this morning through my glasses, and guessed the rest. You are ingenious. Now I understand why you allowed me to escape.

"My love and duty to Catherine, if she still lives; for yourself, my respectful salutations, most admirable of policemen."

It was signed "SILINSKI."

*   *   *   *

I am happy to think that the court-martial held on Lieutenant-Commander George Septimus Marchcourt, on a charge of "neglect of duty, in that he failed to carry out the instructions of his superior officer," resulted in an honourable acquittal for that cheerful young officer. It was an acquittal, which had a far-reaching effect, though at the time it did not promise well.

T. B. was a witness at the trial, which was a purely formal one, in spite of the attention it excited.

T. B. remained at Gibraltar, pending further developments. For the affair of the Nine Men had got beyond Scotland Yard—they were an international problem.

Thanks to the information supplied by Torquet in Brixton prison, supplemented by such particulars as Catherine Silinski was able to supply, the European agents had been arrested. Their trials —if one may anticipate a little—were of the most sensational character, but in no case, whether the investigation was before the gentle tribunals peculiar to English law, or whether they were instituted by the more vigorous courts of France, Germany, or Russia, was the mystery of "Lolo" solved.

But of "Lolo" she had no information to give.

Catherine's evidence, however, was particularly valuable to T. B., not so much because she was able to assist him in his search for the Nine, but from the inside history she was able to give of the working of this colossal organization of crime. We know now the cause of many market "breaks" which were, at the time, inexplicable. We catch a glimpse, in her fascinating story of the method adopted by the Nine, their directors' meetings, to which, apparently, she was admitted.* Catherine appears to have shared the confidence of Meyers, who from time to time confided his fears to her; she knew, intimately, Baggin, and it was through her that Silinski and he met.

T. B. was walking over from La Linea, across the strip of neutral ground which separated Gibraltar from Spain, with young Marchcourt, when he confessed that he despaired of ever bringing the Nine to justice.

"The nations cannot stand the racket much longer," he said; "these Nine Men are costing civilization a million a week! Think of it! A million pounds a week! We must either capture them

*The evidence of Catherine Maria Silinski in relation to the operations of "The Cadiz Conspirators"—Blue Book, 747-11 (Home Office).

soon or effect a compromise. I am afraid they will make peace on their own terms."

"But they must be caught soon," urged the other.

"Why?" demanded T. B. irritably. "Why 'must'. Man, we couldn't catch De Wet in the restricted area of the Orange River Colony; how can we hope to capture one of the fastest war vessels afloat when the men who control her have all the seas to run in?"

"The crew will get tired. After all, they have nothing to gain," persisted the officer; "that is the weakness of their position."

"And their strength," said T. B. "If these men have been persuaded to take the first step in piracy, the rest is easy; if by the promise of huge rewards, they have been induced to put their necks in the noose, the realization of their danger will only make them the more determined to go through with their enterprise."

They had reached the waterport, and T. B. stopped before his hotel.

"Come in," he said suddenly. The two men passed through the paved vestibule and mounted the stair, to T. B.'s room. "I'm going to show you our clue," he said grimly, and extracted from his portfolio the drawing of the little cross with the circular ends.

T. B. himself does not know to this day why he was moved to produce this disappointing little diagram at that moment. It may have been that, as a forlorn hope, he relied upon the application of a fresh young mind to the problem which was so stale in his.

The officer looked and frowned.

"Is that all?" asked Marchcourt, without disguising his disappointment.

"That is all," responded T. B.

They sat looking at the diagram in silence, and T. B., as was his peculiarity, scribbled mechanically on the blotting pad before him.

He drew flowers, and men's heads, and impossible structures of all kinds; he made inaccurate tracings of maps, of columns, pediments, squares, and triangles. Then, in the same absent way, he made a rough copy of the diagram.

Then his pencil stopped and he sat bolt upright.

"Gee!" he whispered.

The young naval officer looked up in astonishment.

"Whew!" whistled T. B.

He jumped up, walked to his trunk, and drew out an atlas.

He turned the leaves, looked long and earnestly at something he saw, closed the book, and turned a little white; but his eyes were blazing.

"I have found 'Lolo'," he said simply.

He took up his pencil and quickly sketched the diagram:

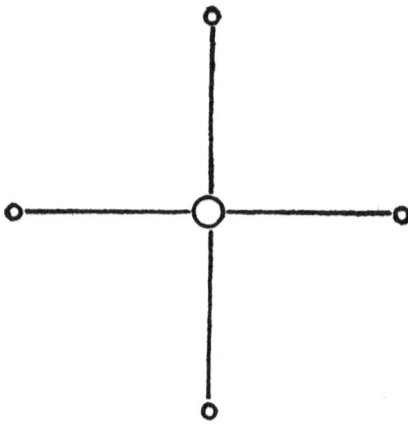

"What that means perhaps our nautical friend will tell us," he said triumphantly, and with a return to his old mannerism.

But young Marchcourt only shook his head.

"Look," said T. B., and added a few letters.

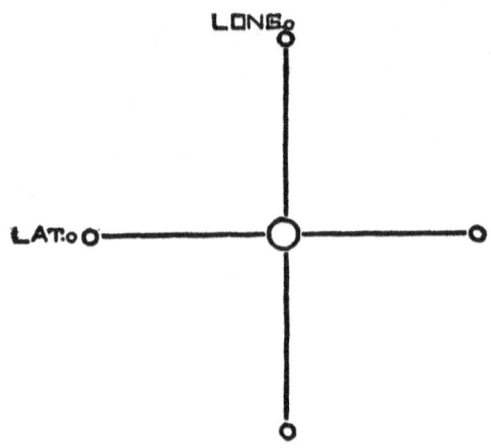

"Longitude nought; latitude nought—L. o, L. o!" whispered the officer. "By Jove! Why, this is off the African coast."

T. B. nodded.

"It is where the Greenwich meridian crosses the equator," he said. "It's 'nowhere'! The only 'nowhere' in the world!"

CHAPTER XXXVI

AT "LOLO"

Under an awning on the quarterdeck of the *Maria Braganza*, George T. Baggin was stretched out in the easiest of easy-chairs in an attitude of luxurious comfort.

"Admiral" Lombrosa, passing on his way to his cabin, smacked him familiarly upon the shoulder—an attitude which epitomized the changed relationships of the pair.

The *Maria Braganza* was steaming slowly eastward, and, since it was the hour of siesta, the deck was strewn with the recumbent forms of men.

Baggin looked up with a scowl.

"Where is Silinski?" he asked, and the other laughed.

"He sleeps, Senor President," said the "Admiral."—there had been some curious promotions on board the *Maria Braganza*—"he is amusing, your Silinski."

Baggin wriggled uncomfortably in his chair, but

made no answer, and the other man eyed him keenly.

Baggin must have felt rather than observed the scrutiny, for suddenly he looked up and caught the sailor's eye.

"Eh?" he asked, as though to some unspoken question. Then, "Where is Meyers?"

Again the smile on the swart face of the Brazilian.

"He is here," he said, as a stout figure in white ducks shuffled awkwardly along the canting deck.

He came opposite to Baggin; and, drawing a chair towards him, with a grunt, he dropped into it with a crash.

"You get fatter and fatter, my friend," said Baggin, regarding the monstrous figure with the interest he would have given to some strange beast.

"Fatter!" gasped the other—ever short of breath was Lucas Meyers—"Course 'm fatter! No exercise—this cursed ship! Oh, what a fool, what a fool I've been!"

He wriggled his big head, and the rolling fat of his neck creased and bulged.

"Forget it," said Baggin. He took a long gold case from his inside pocket, opened it, and selected with care a black cheroot. "Forget it."

"Wish I could! oh, heaven, I wish I could!"
wheezed Meyers. "I'd give half a million to be
safe in the hands of the Official Receiver! I'd give
half a million to be servin' five years in Portland!
Baggin," he said, with comic earnestness, "we've
got to compromise! It's got to be done. Where do
we stand, eh?"

Baggin puffed leisurely at his cigar, but made
no attempt to elucidate the position.

The other man did not wait for any answer. He
wheezed on, whining, complaining, cursing.

Baggin was used to all this; he had had years
of it, but now, with his nerves on edge, this coward-
ice of Meyers' grated.

"I've got an idea, see?" Meyers was saying,
with unwonted eagerness. "I'm a nuisance to you,
ain't I? I know I am. Now, suppose you ventured
into some little port, eh? Put me ashore in a boat.
I'd turn King's evidence—them London murders,
Hyatt an' Moss—it wouldn't do you any harm,
but it'd save me, see? You'd still be at sea; still
be free, eh? I'll make over my share to you—just
enough to get ashore an' live comfortably, if they
let me—"

"Splendid, splendid!" said the silky voice of
Silinski.

Meyers jerked himself erect, with a start.

"Hey!" he breathed. "Hey, Silinski! You go sneakin' about in your bare feet. Don't do it! I hate it, Silinski; it unnerves me. I hate people who come creepin' on a man unawares! That's what you do, Silinski! It's—it's not gentlemanly."

"It is not gentlemanly to talk of deserting your comrades; deserting this ocean republic we have founded," said Silinski gently; "that is treason, high treason."

"Rot!" exploded Meyers. "Rot! Never approved of it; never saw any sense in it! Presidents! Admirals! Citizens! Oaths! Bah!"

The Admiral had walked away to the after-rail.

"Where are the Nine Men of Cadiz?" demanded Meyers, the sweat rolling down his cheeks, a tragic-comic figure. "Where is Bortuski? Where is Morson? Where is Couthwright? Zillier, we know where he is, or was, but where are the others? You an' me, an' this feller Silinski, an' the rest—phutt!" He made a little noise with his mouth. "I know!" he said. He raised a trembling finger accusingly. "They were all here when Silinski came aboard—less'n a week ago."

"My dear man," said Baggin lazily, though his face was white and his lips firm-pressed. "There was the storm——"

"That's a lie!" screamed the fat man, beating

the air with his hands; "that's a lie! The storm didn't take Kohr from his bunk an' leave blood on his pillow! It didn't make Morson's cabin smell of chloroform! I know, I know!"

"There is such a thing as knowing too much," said George T. Baggin, rising unsteadily. "Meyers," he said, "I've been a good friend of yours because I sort of like you in spite of your foolishness. Our friends perished in the storm; it wasn't a bad thing for us, taking matters all round. If this manifesto of ours doesn't secure us a pardon, we can risk making a run for safety. There are fewer of us to blab. See here"—he sat down on the side of the other's chair and dropped his voice— "suppose we can't shock this old world into giving us a free pardon, and the sun gets too warm for us, as it will sooner or later——"

"Suppose it!" Meyers burst in. "D'ye think there's an hour of the day or night when I don't suppose it? Lord! I——"

"Listen, can't you?" said Baggin savagely. "When that happens, what are we to do? We've buried gold on the African coast; we've buried it on the South American coast——"

"All the crew know," grunted the fat man, "we're at the mercy——"

"Wait! wait!" said the other wearily. "Sup-

pose there comes a time when we must make a
dash for safety—with the steam pinnace. Slipping
away in the night when the men of the watch are
doped. You and me, Silinski and the Admiral"—
he bent his head lower—"leaving a time-fuse in
the magazine"—he whispered—"there's a way
out for us, my friend!"

Meyers said nothing. The cold-blooded villainy
of the proposal did not shock him; for a moment
a gleam of hope lit the dark places of his miserable soul.

"But Zillier," he whispered huskily; "we're
going to pick up Zillier; why not leave him?"

"He knows more than any other of our plans,"
said Baggin; "he will be safer with us—for a
time."

"We're going to make one last effort," he went
on, "between here and 'Lolo' we fall in with the
outward bound intermediate Cape mail. It shall
be our last attack upon civilization——"

"Don't do it!" begged Meyers; "for the love of
heaven, don't do it! I can't stand it, Baggin! I
can't stand it!"

He stood on the deck, his feet wide apart, his
big body quivering with fear. Terror gave him a
certain dignity; he was grotesque rather than ridiculous.

"Drop Zillier! Drop everything! Let us clear out——"

Baggin left him babbling and walked to where Silinski strolled with the Captain.

"I've done my best," he said shortly; "he's just mad with fright; there's no backbone in him."

Silinski nodded.

They ate a silent meal in the magnificently upholstered wardroom, which had been converted into a saloon for the officers of the Republic.* After dinner, Silinski and Baggin promenaded the quarter deck together.

"Meyers has gone below," reported the latter in answer to a question; "he got no sleep last night."

"He's a greater danger than any of the others," said Silinski quietly.

They stood for a while watching phosphorescence on the water till Lombrosa's voice recalled them.

"Are you there?" he called quickly. They detected the agitation in his tone and turned together.

"It's Meyers," said the Captain rapidly. "I

*The exact constitution of this extraordinary Republic is not very clear. We have to depend upon the evidence of the warship's crew for such information as we possess, and it would appear that their knowledge was of the slightest.—E. W.

found him in the wireless cabin, trying to send a message. He's half mad.''

''Where is he?'' demanded Silinski, but, before his tongue had formed the words, the voice of the fat man came to him. He came along, the centre of a swaying body of sailors, who held him.

''For God's sake, silence him!'' said the Brazilian hoarsely. ''Don't you hear——''

''Dead! ye'll all be dead!'' yelled Meyers. He was screaming at the top of his voice in English. ''Eh! a time-fuse in your dam' magazine! whilst they get away with the money! Hold 'em! Catch 'em, ye fools!''

At any moment he might remember that the Brazilians who held him could not understand a word he said.

Silinski gave an order, and the struggling man was flung to the deck.

''Murder!'' he screamed. ''Hyatt, an' the other feller! an' poor Morson, an' Kohr. I see the blood on his pillow! an' a time-fuse in the magazine——''

Silinski thrust a handkerchief in his mouth.

''Chloroform,'' he said in Spanish. ''Our friend has been drinking.''

In a few seconds Baggin was back with a bottle of colourless liquid, and a saturated handkerchief was pressed over the struggling man's mouth.

He was silent at last, and, at a word from their Captain, the men who held him released their hold, and went forward to their quarters.

The three men stood in silence, gazing down at the huddled figure. Then, "He must go," said Silinski, and Baggin nodded.

Nobody heard the splash of him as he fell into the water, or heard the one scream of horror that came from his lips as the cold of the water revived him, or saw his large white face staring blankly into the darkness ere he went down to his death.

CHAPTER XXXVII

THE LAST OF THE NINE

To a calm sea, to a dawn all pearl and rose, the crew of the *Maria Braganza* woke. In the night the speed of the warship had been accelerated until she was moving at her top speed, and two columns of black smoke belched from her great funnels. The two men who came on deck at the same moment did not speak one to the other. Baggin was pale; there were dark circles about his eyes; he looked like a man who had not slept. But Silinski was unperturbed to the last.

Dapper, shaven, not unusually pallid, he woke as from a pleasant dream, and appeared on deck trim from point of shoe to finger-nail—a singular man.

All the morning preparations were going on. Ammunition came up from the magazine, dilatory quarter-masters swung out guns; on the masthead was an under-officer armed with a telescope.

He was the principal object of interest to the men on the quarter deck. Every few minutes their eyes would go sweeping aloft.

Beyond the curtest *"bueno dias"* neither the Captain, Baggin, nor the calm Silinski spoke. In Baggin's heart grew a new terror, and he avoided Silinski.

The sun beat down on the stretch of awning that protected the privileged three, but for some reason Baggin did not feel the heat.

He had a something on his mind; a question to ask; and at last he summoned his resolution to put it. He walked over to where Silinski sat reading.

"Gregory," he said—he had never so addressed him before—"is the end near?"

Silinski had raised his eyes when the other had come toward him; he smiled.

"Which variety of end?" he asked.

"There is only one variety," said Baggin steadily. "There is only one thing in the world that counts, and that is life."

"Not money?" sneered the Pole.

"Not money," repeated Baggin; "least of all money."

"You have been reading," said Silinski promptly—it was a point with him that all disturbing thought came as a result of book-reading; "we are at the very beginning of a new life, my friend —look, look!"

From where they stood the man on the main-mast was visible; he was shouting to somebody on the bridge and pointing northward.

"You see?" said Silinski triumphantly, "at the moment of your despair comes the spur to action; throw your philosophies overboard, my friend; they killed Meyers because they developed into fear. We will make our final appeal to the world."

It came reluctantly into view, a big grey-painted steamer with red and black funnels, a great lumbering ocean beast.

Through their glasses the three men watched her, a puzzled frown upon the Captain's face.

"I do not recognize her," he said. "She is larger than the *Ross Castle;* she looks like a gigantic cargo steamer."

"Her decks are crowded with passengers," said Baggin. "I can see women's hats and men in white; what is that structure forward?" He indicated a long superstructure before the steamer's bridge.

"There goes her flag."

A little ball crept up to the mainmast.

"We will show her ours," said the Captain pleasantly, and pushed a button.

Instantly, with a crash that shook the ship,

the forward gun of the *Maria Braganza* sent a shell whizzing through the air.

It fell short and wide of the steamer.

The Captain turned to Silinski as for instructions.

"Sink her," said Silinski.

But the steamer was never sunk.

The little ball that hung at the main suddenly broke, and out to the breeze there floated not the red ensign of the merchant service, but the stars and stripes of America—more, on the little flagstaff at the bow of the ship fluttered a tiny blue flag spangled with stars.

Livid of face, Captain Lombrosa sprang to the wheel.

"It's a Yankee man-o'-war!" he cried, and his voice was cracked. "We've——"

As he spoke the superstructure on the "intermediate," which had excited Baggin's curiosity, fell apart like a house of canvas—as it was—and the long slim barrel of a nine-inch gun swung round.

"Pang!"

The shell carried away a boat and a part of the wireless cabin.

"Every gun!" yelled Lombrosa, frantically

pressing the buttons on the bridge before him.
"We must run for it!"

Instantly, with an ear-splitting succession of
crashes, the guns of the *Maria Braganza* came into
action.

To the last, fortune was with the Nine, for the
second or third shot sent the American over with
a list to starboard.

Round swung the *Maria Braganza* like a frightened hare; the water foamed under her bows as,
running under every ounce of steam, she made her
retreat.

"We must drop all idea of picking up Zillier,"
said Baggin, white to the lips; "this damned warship is probably in wireless communication with
a fleet; can you tap her messages?"

Silinski shook his head.

"The first shell smashed our apparatus," he
said. "What is that ahead?"

Lombrosa, with his telescope glued to his eye,
was scanning the horizon.

"It looks like a sea fog."

But the Captain made no reply.

Over the edge of the ocean hung a thin red haze.
He put the glass down, and turned a troubled face
to the two men.

"In other latitudes I should say that it was a

gathering typhoon," he said. He took another long look, put down the telescope, closed it mechanically, and hung it in the rack.

"Smoke," he said briefly. "We are running into a fleet."

He brought the *Maria Braganza's* bows northward but the smoke haze was there, too.

East, north, south, west, a great circle of smoke and the *Maria Braganza* trapped in the very centre.

Out of the smoke haze grey shadowy shapes, dirty grey hulls, white hulls, hulls black as pitch, loomed into view.

The Captain rang his engines to "stop."

"We are caught," he said.

He opened a locker on the bridge leisurely, and took out a revolver.

"I have no regrets," he said—it was a challenge to fate.

Then he shot himself and fell dead at the feet of the two. Baggin sprang forward, but too late.

"You coward! you coward!" he screamed. He shook his fist in the dead man's face, then he turned like a wild beast on Silinski. "This is the end of it! This is the end of your scheme! Curse you! Curse you!"

He leaped at the Pole's throat.

For a moment they swayed and struggled, then suddenly Baggin released his hold, dropped his head like a tired man, and slid to the deck.

Silinski wiped his knife on the white duck coat of his fallen fellow, and lit a cigar with a hand that did not tremble.

*   *   *   *

One last expiring effort the *Maria Braganza* made: you could almost follow Silinski as he sped from one side of the ship to the other, by the spasmodic shots that came from the doomed ship.

Then four men-of-war—the *Roon*, the *Connecticut*, the *Black Prince*, and the *Gloire*—detached themselves from the encircling fleets and steamed in toward the Brazilian. Shell after shell beat upon the steel hull of the "Mad Battleship," a great hole gaped in her side, her funnels were shot away, her foremast hung limply.

A white flag waved feebly from her bridge and a British destroyer came with a swift run across the smoky seas.

Up the companion-ladder came a rush of marines; and, after them, a revolver in his hand, T. B. Smith, a prosaic Assistant-Commissioner from Scotland Yard.

And the end of this extraordinary story of crime was as commonplace as it could well be.

T. B. came upon Silinski standing with his back to a bulkhead, grimy—bloodstained, but with the butt of a cigar still glowing in the corner of his mouth.

"You are Gregory Silinski," said T. B., and snapped a pair of handcuffs on his wrists. "I shall take you into custody on a charge of wilful murder, and I caution you that anything you now say may be used in evidence against you at your trial."

Silinski said nothing.

www.ingramcontent.com/pod-product-compliance
Lightning Source LLC
Chambersburg PA
CBHW022208010726
47493CB00002B/468